THE TUDOR CHURCH MUSIC OF THE LUMLEY BOOKS

RECENT RESEARCHES IN THE MUSIC OF THE RENAISSANCE

James Haar, general editor

A-R Editions, Inc., publishes six quarterly series—

Recent Researches in the Music of the Middle Ages and Early Renaissance
Margaret Bent, general editor

Recent Researches in the Music of the Renaissance
James Haar, general editor

Recent Researches in the Music of the Baroque Era
Robert L. Marshall, general editor

Recent Researches in the Music of the Classical Era
Eugene K. Wolf, general editor

Recent Researches in the Music of the Nineteenth and Early Twentieth Centuries
Rufus Hallmark, general editor

Recent Researches in American Music
H. Wiley Hitchcock, general editor—

which make public music that is being brought to light
in the course of current musicological research.

Each volume in the *Recent Researches* is devoted
to works by a single composer or to a single genre of composition,
chosen because of its potential interest to scholars and performers,
and prepared for publication according to the standards that govern
the making of all reliable historical editions.

Subscribers to this series, as well as patrons of subscribing institutions,
are invited to apply for information about the "Copyright-Sharing Policy"
of A-R Editions, Inc., under which the contents of this volume
may be reproduced free of charge for study or performance.

Correspondence should be addressed:

A-R EDITIONS, INC.
315 West Gorham Street
Madison, Wisconsin 53703

RECENT RESEARCHES IN THE MUSIC OF THE RENAISSANCE • VOLUME LXV

THE TUDOR CHURCH MUSIC OF THE LUMLEY BOOKS

Edited by Judith Blezzard

A-R EDITIONS, INC. • MADISON

Library of Congress Cataloging in Publication Data
Main entry under title:

The Tudor church music of the Lumley books.

(Recent researches in the music of the Renaissance, ISSN 0486–123X ; v. 65)
Edited from: Ms. partbooks (Royal Appendix 74–76), British Library, London.
1. Choruses, Sacred, Unaccompanied—16th century. 2. Anthems—16th century. 3. Motets—16th century. 4. Part-songs, Sacred—16th century. 5. Music—England—16th century. I. Blezzard, Judith. II. British Library. Manuscript. Royal Appendix 74–76. III. Series.
M2.R2384 vol. 65 [M2081] 84–760227
ISBN 0–89579–147–1

Contents

Preface

The Music

The greater part of the music in the Lumley books (London, British Library Royal Appendix Manuscripts 74–76), compiled between ca. 1547 and ca. 1552, consists of mostly anonymous simple vocal settings of English sacred texts.[1] The remainder, which (judging from the layout and handwriting) was probably compiled somewhat later, consists mainly of anonymous untitled dances set out in score for from two to seven instruments, in simple chordal style. This secular music is not included in the present edition, which consists solely of the twenty-nine sacred pieces forming the first section of each of the three extant partbooks.

The Lumley books constitute one of the most important surviving sources of very early English Reformation church music. They date from a period of upheaval and uncertainty concerning sacred music in England which began around the time of Henry VIII's dissolution of monasteries (ca. 1536–40) and which did not end until after the accession of Elizabeth I in 1558. Many larger monasteries maintained choirs, through which flourished a long-standing tradition of Latin church music by English composers such as Robert Fayrfax, John Taverner, and Thomas Tallis. The forcible dispersal of these choirs at the dissolution seriously disrupted this tradition, since only a few of the monasteries were re-founded as cathedrals in which choral services could continue.[2] It is likely also that many music manuscripts were lost or destroyed. During the reign of Edward VI (1547–53), increasing limitations were placed on sacred music, and the adaptation of Latin music for the English service became a useful expedient, alongside the composition of music especially for the English service. At Mary Tudor's accession, the official reinstatement of Roman Catholicism meant the return to favor of Latin musical settings in the comparatively florid styles of Henry VIII's reign. Music composed for the English service did not readily lend itself to adaptation with Latin texts; consequently, a considerable quantity of music became useless and was therefore destroyed. The Lumley books are one of the few collections to survive this destruction, which eliminated almost all the Protestant church music then in use and much of that in libraries. They are, therefore, of remarkable interest in their representation of early Protestant music.

The Lumley sacred music may be viewed in the following, more specific, historical context. After the dissolution of the monasteries, the call for a simple service which congregations could understand led to the increasing official use of English in the service during the 1540s. Archbishop Cranmer's syllabic musical setting of the Litany in English in 1544 was a significant step in this direction, partly because it exemplified Cranmer's own view that, for the sake of clarity and understanding, musical settings should ideally have only one note to each syllable.[3] Church music epitomizing Cranmer's view thus stood in marked contrast to that of the prevailing Latin tradition in which individual syllables were often set to long and complex melismas. In any case, by the 1540s a tendency towards simplification of this florid style had already arisen, for example in Taverner's shorter masses.[4]

Private devotion among laypeople, as well as congregational worship, came under official scrutiny during this time. The *Primer, set foorth by the Kynges . . . Clergie* of 1545 (largely Cranmer's work) succeeded several previous primers to become the sole permitted version.[5] Practices of metrical private devotion included psalms, at first without music, possibly to be sung to pre-existent popular tunes.[6] The first complete harmonized metrical psalter, for small-scale collective rather than individual devotion, was issued by Robert Crowley in 1549.

The accession of the boy King Edward VI in 1547 was soon followed by severe restrictions on worship and its music. Images, shrines, and so forth were ordered to be removed, and injunctions decreed the discontinuation or simplification of certain musical services, or the substitution of English settings for Latin antiphons. At this stage Cranmer's ideal of syllabic musical settings became a mandate.[7] Only chapels of the royal foundation, such as those at Winchester and Eton, were exempt from these restrictions.[8]

In 1549 the use of the first common prayer book[9] was enforced, to the exclusion of all other service-books for congregational worship except the *Primer, set foorth by the Kynges . . . Clergie*. Because of these edicts no composer would set earlier words to music after this date. John Merbecke's well-known 1550 setting of *The booke of Common praier noted*[10] was dutifully compliant, using monophonic syllabic settings derived partly from plainchant.[11] However, it was made textually obsolete in 1552 by the issue of the second common prayer book,[12] which afforded even less opportunity for musical setting than its predecessor by doing away with certain parts of the Communion service (such as the introit) which could previously have been sung.

Musically the contents of the Lumley books reflect much of the diversity of experiment and accomplishment in English church music which emerged during this period of uncertainty. The simple, almost entirely syllabic style of the Lumley music is in keeping with the required restrictions. In brief, the variety of compositional techniques in the Lumley sacred music shows that the composers had assimilated the somewhat unaccustomed language and the syllabic directness into their style without undue difficulty. In fact, the skill and the means with which the Lumley sacred music composers sought to abide by the official restrictions on church music shows a creative harking-back to earlier traditions, imaginative adaptation of practices of Latin sacred music, and a certain alignment with contemporaneous secular music, all of which makes this music intrinsically as well as historically interesting.

A most obvious means of adapting earlier traditions in this Edwardian era was to set English words to entire pre-existent Latin compositions. This can be seen in the Wanley books, which are roughly contemporary with the Lumley set and are an equally rare repository of this significant Tudor church music tradition.[13] In Wanley may be found two English-language Communion settings which are adaptations of masses by Taverner. As far as can be determined, none of the Lumley pieces is directly adapted from pre-existent Latin music. But the florid imitative contrapuntal style of composers such as Taverner was not abandoned; it was accommodated to the new practices. See, for example, the predominantly imitative writing (within the prescribed syllabic framework) of No. [12] *Magnificat* and the two Nunc Dimittis settings: Nos. [26] and [29]. Not unexpectedly these pieces show a high degree of word repetition. But a simple, slavish reflection of the close-knit imitative style is creatively avoided by periods of homophony.

Particularly successful adaptations of the earlier imitative practices can be seen in Lumley, coincidentally in the few pieces that can be ascribed to known composers. No. [11] *Deus misereatur* is shown by concordances to be the work of Christopher Tye (ca. 1497–ca. 1573), and No. [27] *[Benedictus]* is ascribed in the Lumley books to Tallis (ca. 1505–85). Both Tye and Tallis were active chiefly in Latin church music in the immediate pre-Reformation period, and it is significant that some of their music to English texts—in an imitative style of high quality—was held in sufficient regard for it to appear in the present collection of predominantly much simpler pieces.[14] The simpler homophonic psalm-setting No. [13] *Ne reminiscaris* is also by Tallis, being ascribed to him in concordances. And, on stylistic grounds, No. [25] *[1552 Kyrie]* could well be the work of Tye, but there is no ascription and no known concordance.

The incorporation of plainsong as part of a harmonic texture owes its origin to the cantus firmus technique of some Latin sacred music. This technique of composition occurs in the Lumley music in two ways: first, as the inclusion of an identifiable plainsong given syllabic underlay and used as the Tenor part, and, second, as the allusion to features typical of plainsong rather than to identifiable chants. Most of the Lumley pieces in the first category (i.e., Nos. [3–6], [16], and part of No. [9]) derive their chants from the eight psalm-tones.[15] The pieces fall into verses which sometimes go in pairs, for example, No. [4] *Laudate pueri* Dominum, which is based on the fifth psalm-tone; other pieces show less structural tautness, with verses which are related to each other only by the presence of the chant. See, for example, No. [6] *Iudica me Deus* (based on the eighth psalm-tone). In some pieces the identifiable chant is not used consistently throughout. For example, in No. [16] *Benedictus,* the Tenor chant (in this case the fourth psalm-tone) is readily perceptible in all even-numbered verses, but the Tenor of the remaining verses bears only passing resemblance to this tone. The second, less easily defined category includes pieces in which passages of chant-like melody can be found (not only in the Tenor), and in which the Tenor descends one degree to the final when it might well be expected to rise to the third of the triad.[16] Examples include No. [2] *Te Deum,* measures 1–8, Triplex and No. [19] *Celi enarrant,* measure 34, Tenor. Compliance with official policy is reflected in No. [1] *Litania,* which is based on the chant used by Cranmer for his *Litany* of 1544.

Some of the Lumley pieces have much in common with contemporary English secular vocal music. This compositional technique had its precedent among early metrical psalms, particularly for private or family devotion, in which the texts were intended to be sung to pre-existent popular tunes. The Lumley pieces of this nature (Nos. [15], [17], [18], [20]) are all to metrical texts. They show regular rhythmic patterns and homophonic textures with balanced phrases, stable harmonies, and easily memorable melodies. Despite problems of layout concerning individual pieces (discussed in the Critical Notes below), it seems clear that in most of them fewer than four voice parts prevail for much of the time. No. [18] *Usquequo Domine* and No. [20] *Domine quis* apparently have burdens for the whole ensemble alternating with verses for fewer voices, a feature particularly associated with the fifteenth-century English carol.[17] In most cases it is not possible to determine whether the Lumley pieces of this type are based on pre-existent tunes or whether new tunes were composed which have features reminiscent of contemporary secular music. The exception is No. [17] *Domine Dominus noster,* in which the music of the odd-numbered verses bears a striking resemblance to that of "Blow thy horn, hunter," the well-known piece by William Cornish (d. 1523) in the Henry VIII manuscript (London, British Library Additional Manuscript 31922), which must surely be the origin of the Lumley tune.[18] Although it is for four voices instead of three, the Lumley version is the simpler, and the contrafactum indicates that the emphasis had moved to the top voice instead of the Tenor line upon which Cornish's tune was based. In the Lumley piece, the music of the even-numbered verses always leads back to the opening music of the odd-numbered verses. Thus the music of the even-numbered verses is unlikely to have been derived from a separate piece and could possibly have been adapted from the verse-music (apparently lost) from Cornish's piece.

There are several further pieces in the Lumley books which are less clearly derived from a particular tradition or technique but which nevertheless show consistent verse structure. This is the case with both metrical pieces (for example, No. [14] *Iubilate Deo*) and prose pieces (for example, No. [24] *[Benedicite]*).

The remaining Lumley pieces vary greatly in style, size, and layout. Those near the beginning of the collection are shorter and are on the whole accomplished compositions. Those near the end, although longer and apparently on a grander scale, tend to appear amateurish by comparison. Most of these latter pieces are antiphonal in a predominantly homophonic style; a common feature is higher-pitched repetition enhancing a textual climax, recurrent in No. [23] *[Praised be God],* and in the prayer for Edward VI, No. [22] *[O Lord Christ Jesu].*

A general review of the text sources combined with analysis of scribal practices in the Lumley books shows at least that several of the pieces fall into groups in which all the texts are of a similar date. For example, Nos. [11–24] (exclusive of the metrical pieces and the two prose anthems) were copied by the same group of scribes and have texts dating from ca. 1535 to 1545. Numerous textual alterations in prose pieces in Lumley—particularly those toward the beginning of the collection—serve in general to bring their texts closer to those in the 1549 common prayer book. Nos. [3–10] all have psalm texts similar to those in the 1549 common prayer book. On the other hand, the last five sacred pieces, Nos. [25–29], were copied by a different group of scribes and all have texts from between 1549 and 1552. Derivations of all the metrical texts are identifiable, but the texts themselves have no known source. (The editorial date 1552, ascribed in the present edition of No. [25], reflects the use of this text in the 1552 common prayer book, its earliest appearance in the liturgy. It is likely that this piece was copied in later than the source order suggests, since the scribe was using up spare staves between other pieces.) From the various versions of some texts within the same printed sources, it is clear that differences within a text must have been tolerated, particularly before enforcement of the common prayer book in 1549, thus making exact text dating difficult.

Sources

The Lumley books are the remaining three (Triplex, Contratenor, and Tenor) of a set of four partbooks from which the lowest part, presumably entitled Bassus, is now missing, although it was catalogued as part of the set in 1609.[19] The books may well have originated from a private chapel, probably that of the Fitzalan family at Arundel in Sussex. Between 1552 and 1557 the library at Arundel was merged with that of John, Lord Lumley, who had married Henry Fitzalan's elder daughter, Jane, some time before 1552. By 1556 Fitzalan had moved to Nonesuch (which was at Cheam, Surrey), and the following year Lumley moved there permanently also. During the Edwardian period of upheaval over religion and music it is likely that sung services on a small scale continued in the private chapels of many great families, and it is possible that this reflects the function of the Lumley books. Another possibility is that the Lumley books were in use at the Chapel Royal or Westminster Abbey and came to Arundel together with Thomas Cranmer's library, which Mary Tudor had confiscated at her accession in 1553 and then given to Fitzalan.[20] Unlike the books from Cranmer's library, however, the Lumley books do not bear Cranmer's name. Their importance as historical evidence lies partly in the fact that they were almost certainly used for performance rather than being merely library copies. Whatever their origin, they probably owe their survival not to their sacred content (which became obsolete on Mary Tudor's accession) but to the secular music which was added later, perhaps for members of the Lumley and Fitzalan families.

The books are functional rather than decorative and are visually of no artistic merit. Their condition is fairly good, most of the effects of wear and tear having been repaired. Pen-trials and inscriptions are in many cases decipherable, but apart from the names "Arundell" and "Lumley," it has not been possible to ascribe any significance to them. As far as the sacred music is concerned, only Royal Appendix Manuscript 76, the Tenor book, survives complete. A few leaves are randomly missing from both Royal Appendix Manuscript 74 (the Triplex book) and Royal Appendix Manuscript 75 (the Contratenor book) as well as a substantial portion from the beginning of the latter. Because of the individual layouts of some pieces near the end of the collection, certain Bassus parts have survived. Specific source information is given for each piece in the Critical Notes.

From internal evidence associated with texts, hand,

use of accidentals, and layout, it is certain that the Lumley books were compiled by as many as nine scribes over a number of years. The work was done in two sections, the break occurring after No. [24] *[Benedicite]*. Several of the pieces are joint efforts by up to three scribes. All nine scribes wrote texts; five or six of these nine wrote the music.

Three of the Lumley sacred pieces, No. [11] *Deus misereatur*, No. [13] *Ne reminiscaris*, and No. [28] *[Te Deum]*, have concordances in contemporary and later sources. In the case of No. [28], the sole concordance is with the Wanley books. The layout in Wanley is different, affecting the likely method of performance. (See Critical Notes.) Apart from this, there are only slight differences between the Lumley and Wanley versions. *Deus misereatur* (No. [11]) and *Ne reminiscaris* (No. [13]) have several concordances which are of particular interest, since most of them name the composers. But for both of these pieces the Lumley version is likely to be the earliest to have been composed. The Lumley versions are much shorter and substantially simpler, making it seem as though the subsequent versions were elaborated reworkings, perhaps acceptable under Elizabeth I's aegis but not so under Edward VI's. Because the known concordances of these two Lumley pieces differ in major ways, such as overall length, performing forces, style, and form, they have not served as a resource in preparation of the present edition. Thus, except for the considerations recorded below from Wanley for No. [28], the Lumley books served as the sole source for all pieces in this edition. To facilitate a comparative stylistic analysis, however, there follows a chronological list of concordances of No. [11] *Deus misereatur* and No. [13] *Ne reminiscaris*, given with dates of copying or printing.

Contemporary Concordances

[11] Deus misereatur

1. London, British Library Additional Manuscripts 30480–4—Elizabeth I's reign

2. London, British Library Additional Manuscript 15166—After 1567

3. Shrewsbury, Shropshire County Records Office, SRO 356 Mus. MS 3—Ca. 1597

4. Oxford, Christ Church Library MS 6—Ca. 1625

5. New York, The New York Public Library (Chirk Castle Part-books)— Ca. 1625

6. London, British Library Additional Manuscript 29289—Ca. 1629

7. London, British Library Additional Manuscript 30478—1644

8. Ely, Cathedral Library MS 28 (now in Cambridge University Library)—After 1660

9. James Clifford, *The Divine Services and Anthems usually sung in the Cathedrals and Collegiate Choirs of the Church of England*—(London: William Godbid, 1663)

10. London, British Library Harley Manuscript 7340—1715–20

11. London, British Library Additional Manuscript 30087—1844–46

Concordant sources 1, 2, 6, 7, 10, and 11 are described by Augustus Hughes-Hughes in the *Catalogue of Manuscript Music in the British Museum*,[21] whereas concordant sources 3, 4, 5, 8, and 9 are reported by John Morehen in *Early English Church Music*, volume 19.[22]

[13] Ne reminiscaris

1. London, British Library Additional Manuscript 30513 (The Mulliner Book)—Ca. 1545–ca. 1585

2. John Day, ed., *Certaine notes set forth in foure and three parts . . .*—(London: 1560)

3. John Day, ed., *The whole psalmes in foure partes . . .*—(London: 1563)

4. John Day, ed., *Mornyng and Euenyng prayer and Communion . . .*—(London: 1565)

5. London, British Library Additional Manuscript 29289—Ca. 1629

6. James Clifford, *The Divine Services and Anthems usually sung in the Cathedrals and Collegiate Choirs of the Church of England*—(London: William Godbid, 1663)

7. London, British Library Additional Manuscript 31855—1871

Concordant sources 1, 5, and 7 are described by Hughes-Hughes (see n. 21), whereas the remaining concordances are reported by Daniels and le Huray in *The Sources of English Church Music 1549–1660*.[23]

Modern Editions

Three of the Lumley pieces, Nos. [11], [13], and [27], appear in modern published editions, as follows.

[11] Deus misereatur

The Lumley version has been transcribed by John Morehen in *Christopher Tye: English Sacred Music*, vol. 19 of *Early English Church Music* (London: Stainer and Bell, 1977), 162–92, which also shows an edition of the later, more elaborate version. Similarly, P. C. Buck has an edition of the later version of *Deus misereatur* in Tudor Church Music Octavo Editions (London: Oxford University Press, 1934), no. 73, which is reprinted in *A Sixteenth-Century Anthem Book* rev. ed. (London: Oxford University Press, 1969), 85–88.

[13] Ne reminiscaris

The Lumley version has been edited by Leonard Ellinwood and revised by Paul Doe in *Thomas Tallis: English Sacred Music: Anthems*, vol. 12 of *Early English Church Music* (London: Stainer and Bell, 1973), 111–16, which also, on pp. 43–50, has an edition of the later, more elaborate version. Another elaborated version was the basis for Denis Stevens's edition of *Ne reminis-*

caris in *The Mulliner Book*, vol. 1 of *Musica Britannica* (London: Stainer and Bell, 1951).

[27] [Benedictus]

The Lumley unica version, edited by Judith Blezzard, appears as a supplement to *Musical Times*, 112 (1971): no. 1536. Another edition has been made by Leonard Ellinwood, revised by Paul Doe, and appears in *Thomas Tallis: English Sacred Music: Service Music*, vol. 13 of *Early English Church Music* (London: Stainer and Bell, 1973), 102–19.

Editorial Methods

The Lumley sacred pieces are printed here in the order in which they appear in the source. Although the edition has been prepared as a performance score, the requisite critical apparatus addresses scholarly concerns in reflecting the state of the original source partbooks.

The original partbook names of Triplex, Contratenor, Tenor, and, presumably, Bassus, for the missing fourth book, are preserved here. In comparison with other partbooks surviving from this period, the Lumley books are unusual in that each book contains some music for voices other than that voice by which the book is designated. (See Plate II.) It seems that toward the end of the sacred collection in Lumley the partbooks began to be treated as musical commonplace-books, with additions being made sporadically. The irregular placements in the sources of particular voice lines for Nos. [25], [27], [28], and [29] are reported in the respective Critical Notes. In cases where the source, either by its layout or by scribal cues and directions, infers antiphonal performance, the editorial designations of "Choir I" and "Choir II" are used.

An incipit reflects the clef, key-signature, and mensuration (where present in the source), followed by the first note at manuscript pitch and time-value. Rests are shown in the incipits only in antiphonal pieces where a second group of voices rests before entering for the first time. (See, for example, Nos. [23] and [28].) A broken horizontal bracket above the staff indicates coloration.

All symbols and sections of text or music in brackets have been editorially supplied. Most Bassus parts throughout and occasionally other voice lines (chiefly Contratenor) are editorial reconstructions; these are distinguished by the obvious lack of an incipit. Reconstructions of sections of voice lines are distinguished by brackets.

As far as possible, reconstruction of missing voice lines has been carried out in keeping with the simple harmonic style and texture of the Lumley music, with reference to other similar music and to concordances where appropriate. For the missing Bassus parts there was frequently only one possible solution, especially in homophonic music, for example No. [9]. In imitative pieces such as No. [12] intended points of entry in the Bassus were clear, but detailed comparisons confirmed that imitation in the Bassus soon gave way to a simpler harmonic function. In certain secular-style pieces it was evident from the nature of the Tenor parts at some points that it constituted the harmonic bass of the piece and that no Bassus was required, for example No. [18], measures 1–8. Once the Bassus parts had been editorially established, editorial Contratenor parts were less of a problem, since the music concerned was mostly homophonic and there were few alternative solutions. Missing Triplex music occurring in verse pieces (for example, No. [6], measures 1–40; No. [16], verses 1, 3, and 5) was reconstructed by analogy with Triplex parts of verses surviving complete. No reconstruction was attempted for the portion of No. [1] for which only the Tenor part survives. In this case the possibility of accurate reconstruction was severely limited, and the presentation of a single editorial version from the many which could be postulated in these circumstances seemed pointless. In certain pieces, reconstruction entailed not only the supplying of a missing part but the determination from the layout of the likely method of performance, for example Nos. [15] and [20]. These special problems are discussed in the Critical Notes for each piece.

In this transcription into modern notation, note values have been halved with the aim of providing a notation which the majority of potential users will find convenient. The rhythmic value of final notes has been standardized with a fermata added editorially where necessary. Where a barline appears in any of the source partbooks, a double barline is used in all parts in the edition. But unless specifically stated otherwise, all barlines are editorial. The scribal indication of "bis" is replaced by the standard repeat signs at the point of occurrence and at the end of the phrase. In many cases *signa congruentiae* also seem intended to indicate repeats. In general they have been interpreted as such, but cases of doubt are reported in the Critical Notes.

Accidentals in the present edition conform to modern convention. A sharp or flat meaning natural in the source is so altered without comment, and redundant accidentals have been tacitly omitted. With regard to the complex problems of key-signatures and accidentals, there is little difference in their treatment from the work of one scribe to the next, but most of the copyists show individual inconsistencies—even within the same piece.[24] The problem is exacerbated by uncertainty as to whether an accidental was inserted by the scribe or by a later performer. In general, editorial accidentals have been added only in situations where their use was considered most likely, and with the aim of achieving as high a degree of consistency as was appropriate within each piece. Although a few principles can be postulated, they are tenuous, and the editorial use of accidentals is inevitably based on conjecture rather than on firm conclusions.

The text underlay follows the source as closely as possible, but, since it is far from precise in the source, much of the underlay and its standardization among voice parts, as well as word division, is editorial. Whenever practical, spelling, punctuation, and capitalization have been modernized to conform to the 1928 *Book of Common Prayer*.[25] Obsolete words, however, have been retained where the underlay required, and their meanings are explained in the Critical Notes.[26] The numerous textual alterations which entail a necessary change of length rather than of substance have been made without comment, for example, No. [7], Triplex, measures 1–9, where the original single appearance of the text phrase has been altered in the source to give multiple written-out repetitions. (See Plate I.) Text repeated as a result of the conventional *ij* or :‖: is italicized in the present edition. In the source the text is written out with its music for each verse, rather than all text verses being laid under one statement of the music. The latter format has been adopted in the present edition; cue-size notes and broken slurs indicate the accommodations necessary for performance of subsequent verses.

Notes on Performance

It is likely that the Lumley sacred music was intended for performance on a small scale, possibly by the choir of a private chapel. There is no evidence that instruments took part, although this possibility is not precluded. To judge by the size of the partbooks (28.5 cm. by 19.5 cm.), there were probably no more than two singers per part. The use of boys is unlikely, although No. [25] *[1552 Kyrie]*, for which there is an unusually high Triplex part, may be an exception. However, this and the remaining four final pieces in the collection form a group which was probably copied less systematically than the rest and in which the layouts depart substantially from previous patterns. Much of the music, particularly that near the beginning of the collection, could have been sung by musical members of the household and their friends as part of the kind of family devotion for which the early metrical psalters were intended. In any case, the range finders given at the beginning of each piece will guide the performer on the make-up and distribution of the ensemble voices.

Although the voice parts remain constant for the majority of the pieces, the layout within this varies and sometimes suggests the way in which the music was to be performed. The effects of this on individual pieces are discussed in the Critical Notes, but some general patterns emerge. For example, all the pieces up to and including No. [13] *Ne reminiscaris* are prose pieces with no question of antiphony, but the succeeding group of seven metrical pieces are all either antiphonal or have verse/burden alternation. Three antiphonal prose pieces, No. [22] *[O Lord Christ Jesu]*, No. [23] *[Praised be God]*, and No. [24] *[Benedicite]*, also occur adjacently in the collection. In the antiphonal pieces in the first section of the source, which consists of Nos. [1–24] (see Sources), it would not have been possible for the two groups of singers to be spatially separate, since the equivalent voice parts from each group are written on opposite pages of the same partbook. No single pattern of layout is followed by the remaining five pieces, and, as stated above, there are substantial departures from the voice part for which each book was originally intended.

Critical Notes

The Lumley partbooks, entitled Triplex, Contratenor, and Tenor, (British Library, Royal Appendix Manuscripts 74, 75, and 76) served, with one exception, as the sole source of the present edition. In the case of No. [28] *[Te Deum]*, Bodleian Library Manuscripts Mus. Sch. e. 420 and 422 (hereafter Wanley) were used to supply missing parts, as is detailed below.

In the Critical Notes, the title of each piece is followed by the partbook source (abbreviated here as RA74, RA75, RA76) for each voice and its respective foliation statement. The Critical Notes report all textual and musical variants between the source and the edition which are not otherwise covered by a stated editorial principle. Location of points within each piece is by measure number (m., mm.) and by verse number (v., vv.), where applicable, and then by voice-part name. Pitch identification is as follows: c′ = middle C, c″ = one octave above middle C, and so forth.

Where the layout of an individual piece in the source could affect the manner of its performance, this is explained in a separate paragraph, along with a report of the meaning of obsolete words in the given piece.

[1] Litania

Triplex, RA74 fol. 2r; Tenor, RA76 fols. 2r–3r.

Since barlines are not given in the edition of this piece, each response is numbered for reference. The piece consists of the responses only, to be sung in reply to the priest's petitions. No further reconstruction is possible owing to the absence of all but the Tenor for most of it.

Responses 5, 6, and 7, the direction "8 tymes" appears beneath. Response 12, text torn at note 2. Response 15a, "fulfilled" deleted. Responses 15b and 15c, *signa*, meaning unclear; may indicate permissible omission. Response 16, text torn. Response 20, notes 10–12 are dotted whole-note followed by half-note. Responses 25–29, Tenor, given once with the direction "5 tymes."

[2] Te Deum

Triplex, RA74 fols. 2v–4r; Tenor, RA76 fols. 3v–5r.

M. 20, Tenor, notes 2–3 are a half-note. M. 29, Triplex, note 3 is two half-notes; Tenor, note 2 is two half-notes. Mm. 29–30, Tenor, redundant whole-rest deleted. M. 111, Tenor, note 1 is dotted. Mm. 151–52, Triplex, "ffinis qd" inscribed at end of piece.

[3] De profundis

Triplex, RA74 fols. 4r–4v; Tenor, RA76 fols. 5r–5v.

M. 59, Triplex, redundant half-rest between notes 2 and 3.

[4] Laudate pueri Dominum

Triplex, RA74 fols. 5r–5v; Tenor RA76 fols. 6r–6v.

M. 26, Tenor, "like to the O." M. 40, Triplex, "liftith."

[5] Ecce quam bonum

Triplex, RA74 fol. 5v; Tenor, RA76 fols. 6v–7r.

Mm. 9–38, Triplex, lacking in source. M. 11, note 2 to m. 12, note 1, Tenor, half-note f′ erased but visible. M. 34, Tenor, note 4 has been variously altered including insertion of a redundant half-note c′.

[6] Iudica me Deus

Triplex, RA74 fol. 6r; Tenor, RA76 fols. 7v–8r.

Mm. 1–40, Triplex, lacking in source. M. 60, Triplex and Tenor, *signa* over note 2.

[7] Omnes gentes

Triplex, RA74 fols. 6r–7r; Tenor, RA76 fols. 8v–9r.

M. 20, Triplex and Tenor, "upon" under notes 1–2 deleted. M. 21, Tenor, note 2 is whole-note. M. 27, Tenor, note 5 is whole-note. M. 47, Triplex and Tenor, note 1 has "3" beneath.

[8] Non nobis Domine

Triplex, RA74 fols. 7r–8v; Contratenor, RA75 fol. 1r; Tenor, RA76 fols. 9v–10r.

Mm. 1–62, Contratenor, lacking in source. M. 5, Tenor, E-flat of key signature omitted. M. 17, Triplex and Tenor, beats 3 and 4, half-note and two quarter-notes to the text "mouthis and." M. 21, Tenor, E-flat in key signature. Mm. 26–29, Tenor, E-flat of key signature omitted. M. 30, Triplex, E-flat in key signature. M. 35, Triplex, E-flat in key signature omitted. M. 68, note 4 to m. 71, note 1, Contratenor and Tenor, rhythm is half-note, two quarter-notes, two half-notes, two quarter-notes, half-note, whole-note. M. 80, Contratenor and Tenor, rhythm is dotted half-note, quarter-note, two half-notes, to the text "Father to the."

[9] Deus in nomine tuo

Triplex, RA74 fols. 9r–9v; Contratenor, RA75 fols. 1v–2r; Tenor, RA76 fols. 11r–11v.

M. 72, Triplex, source text damaged and missing; "bis" or *signum* illegible but repeat editorially supplied by analogy with other voice parts.

[10] Voce mea

Triplex, RA74 fols. 9v–10v; Contratenor, RA75 fols. 2r–3r; Tenor, RA76 fols. 11v–12r.

M. 48, Triplex, closing "bis" cue lacking but editorially supplied by analogy with other voice parts.

[11] Deus misereatur [Christopher Tye]

Triplex, RA74 fols. 10v–11r; Contratenor, RA75 fols. 3r–4r; Tenor, RA76 fols. 12v–13r.

M. 8, note 2—m. 10, note 1, Contratenor, inserted on extra staff to accommodate limited space. M. 17, Triplex, note 1 is sharped. Mm. 21–28, Triplex, inserted on extra staff.

[12] Magnificat

Triplex, RA74 fols. 11v–12v; Contratenor, RA75 fols. 4r–5v; Tenor, RA76 fols. 13v–14v.

M. 9, Contratenor, E-flat of key signature is lacking. M. 23, Contratenor, E-flat in key signature. M. 27, Contratenor, note 2 has fermata. M. 30, Contratenor, E-flat of key signature omitted. M. 33, Contratenor, E-flat in key signature. M. 50, Contratenor, E-flat of key signature omitted. M. 69, Contratenor, note 1, extraneous b deleted. M. 94, Triplex, note 1 has natural. M. 132, Triplex, beat 2 is erroneous half-note. M. 144, Triplex, notes and text inserted.

[13] Ne reminiscaris [Thomas Tallis]

Triplex, RA74 fol. 13r; Contratenor, RA75 fols. 5v–6r; Tenor, RA76 fol. 15r.

M. 22, Contratenor, note 1 is whole-note. Mm. 22–54, Contratenor, key signature is lacking. M. 46, Triplex, has erroneous sharp inflection. M. 52, Tenor, has fermata. Mm. 52–53, Contratenor, barline. M. 53, Tenor, whole-note.

[14] Iubilate Deo

Triplex, RA74 fol. 13v; Contratenor, RA75 fols. 6v–7r; Tenor, RA76 fols. 15v–16r.

In RA75 and RA76 the verses follow the normal succession, but the layout of the surviving portion of the piece in RA74, in which only odd-numbered verses appear on a verso page, suggests antiphonal performance. In any case, the antiphonal layout of RA74 does not necessarily preclude successive performance of the verses by the same singers, and this, in fact, seems more likely to have been the manner of performance, if the layout of RA75 and RA76 is correct. "So be it" is sung only at the end of the whole piece. M. 13, v. 1, all voices, "sprite" means "spirit."

M. 10, v. 1, Tenor, E-flat of key signature omitted to end of piece. M. 10, vv. 1 and 2, Tenor, note 3 lacks sharp. M. 17, v. 2, Tenor, note 3, sharp lacking; vv. 2, 4, and 5, Triplex, lacking in source.

[15] Benedicite

Contratenor, RA75 fols. 7v–9r; Tenor, RA76 fols. 16v–18r.

This piece may have had a Triplex part also since at least one leaf is missing at this point in RA74. It appears likely from the layout that the music up to m. 40 was sung antiphonally, with the remainder of the piece sung by the whole ensemble even though the rest values, as reported below, do not accurately reflect this. The other option of the apparently antiphonal music forming a burden between the remaining verses is unlikely as this would disrupt the text and lengthen the piece to no purpose.

M. 21, Tenor, Choir I, double whole-rest missing. M. 22, Contratenor and Tenor, Choir I, *signum* meaning is unclear. M. 39, Contratenor, Choir II, double whole-rest missing; Tenor, Choir II, two double whole-rests missing; Contratenor and Tenor, Choir I, *signum* meaning is unclear. Preceding m. 40, vv. 3 and 4, Tenor, seventeen double whole-rests are redundant. M. 50, v. 5, Tenor, the text "Holy and" set to two quarter-notes followed by a half-note; v. 6, Contratenor and Tenor, the text "thorow" set to two quarter-notes.

[16] Benedictus

Triplex, RA74 fols. 14r–15r; Contratenor, RA75 fols. 9v–11r; Tenor, RA76 fols. 18v–20r.

The layout in RA75, RA76, and the surviving portion of the piece in RA74, with odd-numbered verses on verso pages and even-numbered verses on recto pages, suggests antiphonal performance of all verses until the tenth, which appears on both verso and recto pages. This, together with the presence of divisi notes in the final cadence, makes it likely that v. 10 was sung simultaneously by the whole ensemble. M. 19, v. 6, "hight" means "be called." M. 22, v. 8, "trade" means "course," "way."

Triplex starts at v. 2; vv. 1, 3, and 5 presumed to be on missing leaf. M. 15, v. 7, Triplex, sharp lacking. M. 20, vv. 4 and 6, Contratenor, note 5 lacks sharp. M. 22, v. 2, Triplex, c′ lacks sharp. M. 24, v. 2, all voices, whole-rest in this verse only; vv. 4, 6, and 8 have the correct half-rest. M. 25, v. 2, all voices, the text "mouthis" set to dotted half-note followed by a quarter-note. M. 29, v. 4, Triplex, note 1 is e′. Mm. 38–40, Contratenor, v. 10, text is given twice in the source, on fol. 10v set to c′-sharp, d′, c′-sharp, and on fol. 11r set to e′, f′, e′; Tenor, v. 10, is likewise given twice (on fols. 19v and 20r), but both cases are identical, as shown here.

[17] Domine Dominus noster

Triplex, RA74 fols. 15v–17r; Contratenor, RA75 fols. 12r–14v; Tenor, RA76 fols. 20v–22v.

The layout, in which odd-numbered verses appear on verso pages and even-numbered verses on recto pages, suggests antiphonal performance. M. 28, all voices, "impery" means "supreme rule" or "authority."

M. 1, v. 3, all voices, the text "mouthis of" set to a half-note followed by two quarter-notes. M. 2, v. 1, all voices, the text "thorow" set to two quarter-notes. M. 7, vv. 3, 5, 7, and 9, Triplex, sharp lacking on beat 4. M. 14, v. 4, Triplex, note on beat 3 is lacking. M. 15, v. 10, all voices, the text "thorow" set to two quarter-notes. M 16, vv. 6, 8, and 10, Contratenor, note 2 is b. M. 20, v. 10, Contratenor, the text "every" set to two quarter-notes followed by a half-note. M. 23, v. 10, Triplex, note 1 lacks sharp. M. 25, vv. 2, 4, 6, and 8, Triplex, note 1, sharp lacking.

[18] Usquequo Domine

Triplex, RA74 fol. 19v; Contratenor, RA75 fols. 14v–15v;.Tenor, RA76 fols. 22v–23v.

The Triplex part consists of vv. 1 and 6 only. The Contratenor and Tenor parts give all verses, including the first verse twice to different music. It seems clear that the second setting of v. 1, together with the Triplex and lost Bassus for this verse, provide a burden to be sung between subsequent verses. V. 6 presents a problem inasmuch as the Tenor music does not fit with that of the Triplex and Contratenor. Probably, therefore, two alternative methods of performance for v. 6 were envisaged: one in which it was sung by Contratenor and Tenor alone, and the other in which v. 6 was sung by Triplex, Contratenor, and Bassus only as a doxology to the piece. M. 3, v. 2, all voices, "lade" means "load oppressively."

M. 1, v. 6, Contratenor, "We praise" instead of "Praise we"; vv. 2–6, Tenor, note 2 lacks sharp. M. 3, vv. 2, 3, 4, and 6, Contratenor, note 1 lacks flat; Contratenor and Tenor, text replaces "no help come of thee" (deleted); vv. 1, 3, and 6, Tenor, note 4 lacks flat. M. 8, Tenor, *signum*. M. 11, Triplex, text replaces "shall no help come from thee" (deleted). M. 20, Triplex, *signum*.

[19] Celi enarrant

Triplex, RA74 fols. 17v–19r; Contratenor, RA75 fols. 16v–18r; Tenor, RA76 fols. 24v–26r.

The layout, in which odd-numbered verses appear on verso pages and even-numbered verses on recto pages in all three part-books, suggests antiphonal performance by two groups which at no time sing together.

M. 7, vv. 3 and 5, Triplex, note 1, E-flat of key signature omitted. M. 7, v. 1, Triplex, note 3, E-flat of key signature omitted; vv. 5 and 7, Tenor, note 2, E-flat of key signature omitted; vv. 1 and 3, Tenor, note 4, E-flat of key signature omitted. M. 9, v. 7, Contratenor, note 1 lacks flat. M. 11, vv. 1 and 3, Triplex, note 3 lacks flat; vv. 3, 5, and 7, Tenor, note 4 lacks sharp. M. 12, vv. 5 and 7, Tenor, final note is whole-note, a; v. 1, Tenor, final note lacks sharp. M. 13, v. 5, Triplex and Tenor, final syllables "-nu-eth" set to two quarter-notes. M. 14, vv. 1, 5, and 7, sharp lacking on note 1. M. 16, vv. 1, 3, and 7, Triplex, sharp lacking. M. 17, Triplex and Tenor, at the beginning of the even-numbered verses, one-flat key signature. M. 20, v. 6, Tenor, pitches are b, b, b. M. 22, v. 6, Contratenor, note 2 lacks sharp. M. 23, v. 6, Contratenor, sharp on note 2 but lacking on note 1. M. 25, v. 2, all voices, text "thorough" set to dotted half-note followed by quarter-note. M. 29, v. 4, Tenor, "mynds" (deleted) also on note 1. M. 30, v. 8, all voices, *signum*, possibly indicating repetition of mm. 30–34.

[20] Domine quis

Choir I: Contratenor, RA75 fols. 18v–20r; Tenor, RA76 fols. 26v–28r. Choir II: Triplex, fol. 20r; Contratenor, RA75 fol. 20r; Tenor RA76 fol. 28r.

In RA75 and RA76 all eight verses are set out successively; then follows a passage consisting of two rest groups of large value on either side of the passage "Lord, who is he," followed by a different setting of the text of v. 1. RA74 has a setting of v. 1 only. The present edition reflects the probability that all the verses were sung by Contratenor and Tenor alone with all four voices singing the added setting of v. 1 (mm. 14–26 in the present edition) as a burden. The presence of the rest-values surrounding the passage "Lord, who is he" in the burden suggests its possible interpolation during the verses for Contratenor and Tenor (as is done in the present edition). Although the passage could stand alone, it is not entirely satisfactory harmonically and, therefore, Triplex and Bassus parts have been editorially supplied. It is difficult to see what further material could have been used to fill the corresponding gap in the burden (mm. 23–24 in the present edition), and so the same passage has been editorially interpolated. A performance of the work would need six singers, although if the interpolation in the burden were performed antiphonally, as seems probable, eight singers would be required. M. 6, v. 3, all voices, "ruth" means "mischief," "calamity," "ruin." M. 8, v. 3, all voices, "smart" means "grief," "sorrow," "affliction." M. 13, v. 7, all voices, "shift" means "fraud" or "evasive device."

Mm. 23–24, all voices show rests, Triplex and Tenor of the correct value, but Contratenor lacks a whole-rest.

[21] [O Lord, rebuke me not]

Triplex, RA74 fols. 20v–22r; Contratenor, RA75 fols. 20v–22r; Tenor, RA76 fols. 28v–30r.

M. 84, all voices, "woodness" means "mental derangement," "insanity."

Mm. 26–27, Contratenor, notes unclear, underlaying incomplete. M. 29, Triplex, "have mercy on" deleted. M. 50, Tenor, key signature omitted. M. 60, Tenor, one-flat key signature. M. 64, Triplex, two whole-rests redundant; Tenor, key signature omitted. M. 88, Tenor, one-flat key signature. M. 96, Tenor, key signature omitted. M. 118, Contratenor, note 4 has fermata. M. 119, Triplex, change to mezzo-soprano C clef. Mm. 144–45, all voices, Φ. M. 149, Tenor, note 3, b, deleted and replaced by c′ in the source. M. 158, all voices, after note 2, ¢.

[22] [O Lord Christ Jesu]

Choir I: Triplex, RA74 fols. 22v–23v; Contratenor, RA75 fols. 22v–23v; Tenor, RA76 fols. 30v–31v. Choir II: Triplex, RA74 fols. 23r–24r; Contratenor, RA75 fols. 23r–24r; Tenor, RA76 fols. 31r–32r.

The layout indicates antiphonal singing by two groups who also occasionally sing together.

M. 10, Contratenor, Choir II, whole-note followed by half-note. Mm. 17–19, Tenor, Choir II, torn. Mm. 30–33, Tenor, Choir I, two redundant half-rests. M. 39, Triplex, Choir II, half-rest missing. M. 40, note 2–m. 41, note 4, Tenor, Choir II, torn. Mm. 45–46, Tenor, Choir II, dotted half-note, quarter-note, five half-notes. M. 49, Triplex, Choir I, half-rest missing. M. 55, Contratenor, Choir I, half-rest missing. M. 60, Triplex, Choir I, two double whole-rests missing. M. 91, Tenor, Choir I, II, note 2 has fermata. M. 94, note 5–m. 95, note 1, Tenor, Choir I, torn. M. 96, Contratenor, Choir I, redundant half-rest. M. 100, Tenor, Choir II, redundant half-rest. M. 103, Contratenor, Choir I, text "thorough thy" set to two eighth-notes followed by quarter-note. M. 110, Tenor, Choir II, two half-notes. M. 115, Tenor, Choir I, one whole-rest and one half-rest missing. M. 115, Triplex and Contratenor, Choir I, II, Φ. M. 123, Tenor, Choir I, note 3 has fermata. M. 128, Triplex, Choir II, and Contratenor, Choir I, C; Triplex, Choir I, ¢. M. 139, Contratenor, Choir II, note 3 lacks sharp.

[23] [Praised be God]

Choir I: Triplex, RA74 fol. 24v; Contratenor, RA75 fol. 24v; Tenor, RA76 fol. 32v. Choir II: Triplex, RA74 fol. 25r; Contratenor, RA75 fol. 25r; Tenor, RA76 fol. 33r.

The layout indicates antiphonal singing by two groups who also occasionally sing together.

Mm. 17 and 19, all voices, Choir II, "unryghtwyse." Mm. 20–21, all voices, Choir I, six redundant whole-rests. Mm. 25–29, all voices, Choir I, "ryghtwysnes." Mm. 36–37, Contratenor and Tenor, Choir I, nine redundant whole-rests. Mm. 36–37, Triplex, Choir I, five redundant whole-rests. M. 50, Triplex, Choir I, note 4 is set to "our" instead of "and." M. 52, Contratenor, Choir I, has a, and Contratenor, Choir II, has c'. Mm. 54–55, Triplex, Choir I, "father" instead of "O Lord." M. 60, Tenor, Choir II, note 3 is dotted half-note followed by quarter-note. M. 67, Tenor, Choir II, note 4 is lacking. Mm. 70–71, Tenor, upper notes of divisi in Choir I, lower notes in Choir II. Mm. 71–72, Contratenor, upper notes in Choir I, lower notes in Choir II.

[24] [Benedicite]

Choir I: Triplex, RA74 fols. 25v–27v; Contratenor, RA75 fols. 25v–27v; Tenor, RA76 fols. 33v–35v. Choir II: Triplex, RA74 fols. 26r–28r; Contratenor, RA75 fols. 26r–28r; Tenor, RA76 fols. 34r–36r.

The layout indicates antiphonal singing by two groups who also occasionally sing together.

M. 10, note 2–m. 11, Tenor, Choir II, torn. M. 23, Tenor, Choir II, torn. M. 24, Triplex, Choir I, "all" under note 4 deleted. M. 29, all voices, Choir II, time signature 3 is given. M. 53, Tenor, Choir II, dotted half-note, quarter-note, double whole-note with fermata to the word "evermore." Mm. 54–55, Triplex, Choir I, written a third too low. M. 79, Triplex, Choir II, "Ye" under note 1 deleted. Mm. 114–end, Triplex, Choir I, note 1, B-flat in key signature. Mm. 118–end, Triplex, Choir II, note 1, B-flat in key signature.

[25] [1552 Kyrie]

Triplex, RA74 fol. 27r; Contratenor RA75 fol. 27r; Tenor, RA76 fol. 35r.

The Triplex and Contratenor parts are untexted in the source.

M. 2, Tenor, notes 1 and 2 are g. M. 12, Tenor, notes 1 and 2 are g.

[26] [Nunc dimittis]

Triplex, RA74 fols. 27v–28r; Contratenor, RA75 fols. 27v–28v; Tenor, RA76 fols. 35v–36v.

M. 8, Contratenor, note 1 is a. M. 15, Tenor, notes 1 and 2 are a whole-note, b. M. 20, Triplex, note 1 is c''. M. 37, Triplex, rests replace illegible deleted notes over the text "Israell." M. 46, Triplex, note 1 is a'. M. 50, Contratenor, note 4 is d'. Mm. 55–57, Tenor, written a fourth too low.

[27] [Benedictus] [Thomas] Tallis

Primus contratenor, RA75 fols. 29v–31v; Secundus contratenor, RA75 fols. 30r–32r; Tenor, RA76 fols. 37v–39v; Bassus, RA76 fols. 38r–40r.

The upper two voice parts in this piece are labeled "Contratenor parte secundus" and "Primus contratenor parte."

M. 2, Secundus contratenor, word lacking. M. 37, Tenor, notes 1 and 2 are dotted. Mm. 45–46, Tenor, text lacking. M. 51, Secundus contratenor, note 1 is dotted. M. 59, Secundus contratenor, notes 1 and 2 are b. M. 60, Tenor, note 1 is c. M. 73, Tenor, "our" instead of "the." M. 95, Secundus contratenor, word omitted. M. 116, Primus contratenor, note 2 is b. Mm. 116–17, Tenor, underlay insufficient.

[28] [Te Deum]

Choir I: Triplex, RA75 fols. 32v–33v; Contratenor, RA75 fols. 33r–34r; Tenor, Bodleian Library MS Mus. Sch. e. 420 fols. 80r–82r; Bassus, Bodleian Library MS Mus. Sch. e. 422 fols. 78v–80v. Choir II: Triplex, RA74 fols. 28v–29v; Contratenor, RA74 fols. 29r–30r; Tenor, RA76 fols. 41r–42r; Bassus, RA76 fols. 40v–41v.

Whereas the Bodleian source (Wanley) is set out in only four continuous parts which occasionally divide, the Lumley source is clearly set out for antiphonal performance by two groups, each of four voices, which (unlike the antiphonal groups in other pieces in this source) could be spatially separate, perhaps in cantoris and decani fashion. Probably because the Wanley version is not antiphonal, there is no repetition of the portion beginning "Holy, holy, holy." In the Lumley source, the rest-groups for one choir are always four whole-notes in length, irrespective of the amount of music being sung by the other choir. Accurate notation of the rest-groups would have been unnecessary, as it is obvious when a cadence in one choir is imminent, from which the other choir would receive its cue.

M. 31, Tenor, Choir I, note 4 is e'. M. 63, Triplex, Choir I, B-flat in key signature. M. 65, Contratenor, Choir II, change to tenor C clef. M. 67, Tenor, Choir II, note 1 is half-note and note 2 is d'. M. 74, Tenor, Choir I, note 2 is g. M. 88, all voices, Choir II, text "shalbe" set to a single half-note. M. 95, Contratenor, Choir I, note 1 is d'. M. 95, note 2–m. 96, note 1, Contratenor, Choir I, lacking. M. 96, Contratenor, Choir I, notes 2 and 3 are b, b. M. 101, Tenor, Choir II, note 1 is lacking. M. 116, Triplex, Choir I, note 2 lacks dot in Wanley. M. 117, Triplex, Choir I, note 1 lacks dot in Wanley; Contratenor, Choir I, whole-note; Tenor and Bassus, Choir I, lack dot. M. 122, Tenor, Choir II, note 3, half-note, note 4 is b. M. 130, Triplex, Choir I, note 3 is dotted whole-note. M. 131, Triplex, Choir I, rest is lacking. Mm. 134–35, Tenor, whole-note.

[29] [Nunc dimittis]

Triplex, RA76 fol. 43r; Contratenor, RA75 fol. 34v;

Tenor, RA74 fol. 30v and RA76 fol. 42v; Bassus, RA74 fol. 31r.

The layout suggests that this music was intended for double choir. It is likely that a leaf missing at this point from RA75 contained the Triplex part, and that the missing book contained the Contratenor and Bassus parts. The Tenor parts, both of which survive, are virtually identical throughout, and the piece is self-sufficient in the four parts which survive. Thus the other parts, like the Tenors, were probably in matching pairs, perhaps laid out to reflect the order in which the choir may have stood.

M. 48, Tenor, source has two half-notes instead of whole-note.

Acknowledgments

The following libraries have kindly permitted use of their manuscripts for this edition: the British Library, London, England (Royal Appendix Manuscripts 74–76), and the Bodleian Library, Oxford, England (Manuscripts Mus. Sch. e. 420–22). In my graduate thesis (from which the present edition developed) I have acknowledged the help of several individuals, but my greatest debt of gratitude is to Dr. Richard Rastall, Senior Lecturer in Music at the University of Leeds, who supervised and assisted me throughout the preparation of most of this work.

Judith Blezzard

Notes

1. A full survey can be found in Judith Blezzard, "The Sacred Music of the Lumley Books (British Museum Royal Appendix Manuscripts 74–76): An Edition and Critical Study" (Ph.D. diss., University of Leeds, 1972). A brief summary with facsimile appears in Judith Blezzard, "The Lumley Books: A Collection of Tudor Church Music," *Musical Times* 112 (1971): 128–30.

2. For a detailed account of the musical effects of the dissolution, see Peter le Huray, *Music and the Reformation in England* (London: Herbert Jenkins, 1967), 1–30.

3. Cranmer's well-known letter of 1545 to Henry VIII on this matter is given in William Oliver Strunk, ed., *Source Readings in Music History from Classical Antiquity through the Romantic Era* (London: Faber, 1950), 350–51.

4. le Huray, *Music and the Reformation,* 140–41; also Hugh Benham, *Latin Church Music in England 1460–1575* (London: Barrie and Jenkins Ltd., 1977), 164.

5. *The primer, set foorth by the Kynges maiestie and his Clergie* (London, 1545).

6. Erik Routley, *The Music of Christian Hymnody* (London: Independent Press, 1957), 36.

7. For example, see the injunctions to the Dean and Chapter of Lincoln Cathedral in 1548, quoted in le Huray, *Music and the Reformation,* 9.

8. Frank L. Harrison, "Church Music in England," in *The Age of Humanism 1540–1630,* ed. Gerald Abraham, vol. 4 of *The New Oxford History of Music* (London: Oxford University Press, 1968), 466.

9. *The booke of the common prayer* (London: Richard Grafton, 1549).

10. John Merbecke, *The booke of Common praier noted* (London: Richard Grafton, 1550).

11. Merbecke composed polyphonic Latin and English church music, printed in P. C. Buck et al., eds., *Tudor Church Music* (London: Oxford University Press, 1929), 10:155–227, and was the author of several considerable theological works, discussed in R. A. Leaver, *The Work of John Marbeck* (Oxford: Sutton Courtenay Press, 1978).

12. *The Boke of Common prayer* (London: Edward Whitchurch, 1552).

13. le Huray, *Music and the Reformation,* 173–75. The Wanley books are Oxford, Bodleian Library Manuscripts Mus. Sch. e. 420–22.

14. Tye's Latin church music is in *Christopher Tye: The Latin Church Music,* ed. John Satterfield, Recent Researches in the Music of the Renaissance, vols. 13 and 14 (Madison: A-R Editions, Inc., 1972). Tallis's Latin church music is in Buck et al., eds., *Tudor Church Music* (London: Oxford University Press, 1928), vol. 6, and is discussed in Paul Doe, *Tallis,* rev. ed. (London: Oxford University Press, 1976).

15. Benedictines of Solesmes, ed., *Liber usualis* (Tournai: Desclée, 1961), 112–17.

16. Discussed further in John Aplin, "The Survival of Plainsong in Anglican Music: Some Early English Te Deum Settings," *Journal of the American Musicological Society* 32 (1979): 247–75.

17. For examples, see John Stevens, ed., *Medieval Carols,* Musica Britannica, vol. 4 (London: Stainer and Bell, 1952).

18. Transcribed in John Stevens, ed., *Music at the Court of Henry VIII,* Musica Britannica, vol. 18, no. 35 (London: Stainer and Bell, 1962).

19. Sears Jayne and Francis R. Johnson, eds., *The Lumley Catalogue of 1609* (London, 1956), 286.

20. Jane A. Bernstein, "The Chanson in England 1530–1640: A Study of Sources and Styles" (Ph.D. diss., University of California, Berkeley, 1974), 97.

21. Augustus Hughes-Hughes, *Catalogue of Manuscript Music in the British Museum* (London: British Museum, 1906), 1: passim.

22. John Morehen, ed., *Christopher Tye: English Sacred Music,* vol. 19 of *Early English Church Music* (London: Stainer and Bell, 1977), 332–34. Variants among the versions other than the Lumley one are given here.

23. Ralph T. Daniels and Peter le Huray, *The Sources of English Church Music 1549–1660* (London: Stainer and Bell, 1972), 2: 143.

24. This matter is discussed further in Judith Blezzard, "Editing Early English: Some Further Evidence," *Musical Times* 119 (1978): 265–68.

25. *The Book of Common Prayer, with the Additions and Deviations Proposed in 1928,* (London: Eyre and Spottiswoode, 1928).

26. *The Oxford English Dictionary* (1933; reprint, Oxford: Claredon Press, 1970).

Plate I. No. [6] *Iudica me Deus* and the opening of No. [7] *Omnes gentes* in the Triplex partbook.
Royal Appendix MS 74, fol. 6r. Original size: 27.9 cm. x 18.7 cm.
(By permission of the British Library)

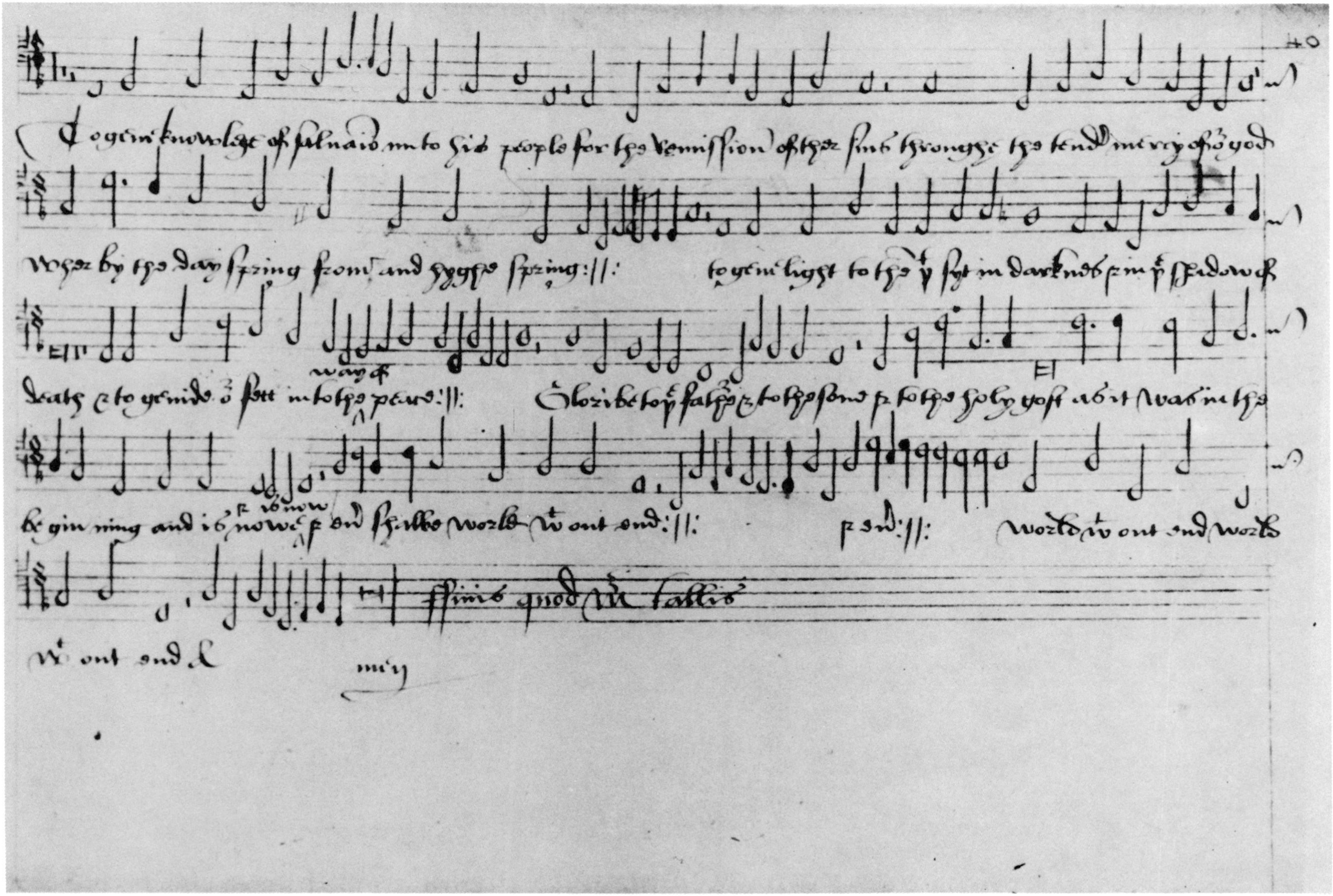

Plate II. No. [27] *[Benedictus]*, mm. 82ff of the Bassus part in the Tenor partbook.
Royal Appendix MS 76, fol. 40r. Original size: 27.9 cm. x 18.7 cm.
(By permission of the British Library)

THE TUDOR CHURCH MUSIC OF THE LUMLEY BOOKS

[1] Litania

Tenor
1
O God the Fa- ther of heav- en: have mer- cy up- on us mis- er- a- ble sin- ners.
2
O God the Son, Re- deem- er of the world: have mer- cy up- on us mis- er-
3
- a- ble sin- ners. O God the Ho- ly Ghost, pro- ceed- ing from the Fa- ther and the Son:
4
have mer- cy up- on us mis- er- a- ble sin- ners. O ho- ly, bless- ed, and glo- ri-
- ous Trin- i- ty, three per- sons and one God: have mer- cy up- on us mis- er- a- ble
5
6
7
sin- ners. Spare us, good Lord. Good Lord, de- liv- er us. We be-seech thee to hear us, good Lord.
8
9
10
Son of God: we be-seech thee to hear us. Grant us thy peace. Have mer- cy up- on us.
11
12
13
O Christ, hear us. Lord, [have] mer- cy up- on us. Christ, have mer- cy up- on us.
14
15
Lord, have mer- cy up- on us. O our Fa- ther, which art in heav- en,
15a
Hal-low- ed be thy Name. Thy king- dom come. Thy will be done, in earth as it is
in heav- en. Give us this day our dai- ly bread, our dai- ly bread, give us
this day our dai- ly bread. And for- give us our tres- pass- es. As we for- give them

which tres- pass a- gainst us. And let us not be led in- to temp- ta- ti- on,
in- to temp- ta- ti- on; but de- liv- er us, but de- liv- er us from all e- vil:
15b
for thine is the king- dom, and the power and the glo- ry, For ev- er.
15c
[Al- ways so] be it.
16
Triplex
[Contratenor]
Tenor
[Bassus]
17
O Lord, a- rise, help us, and de- liv- er us for thine hon- our.
18
O Lord, a- rise, help us, and de- liv- er us for thy Name's sake.
19
Al- ways so be it.
20
Gra- ci- ous- ly look up- on our af- flic- ti- ons.
21
Mer- ci- ful- ly

22
for-give the sins of thy peo- ple. O Son of Da- vid, have mer- cy up- on us.
for-give the sins of thy peo- ple. O Son of Da- vid, have mer- cy up- on us.
for-give the sins of thy peo- ple. O Son of Da- vid, have mer- cy up- on us.
for-give the sins of thy peo- ple. O Son of Da- vid, have mer- cy up- on us.
23
Gra- ci- ous- ly hear us, O Christ; gra- ci- ous- ly hear us, O Lord Christ.
Gra- ci- ous- ly hear us, O Christ; gra- ci- ous- ly hear us, O Lord Christ.
Gra- ci- ous- ly hear us, O Christ; gra- ci- ous- ly hear us, O Lord Christ.
Gra- ci- ous- ly hear us, O Christ; gra- ci- ous- ly hear us, O Lord Christ.
24
25
26
As we do put our trust in thee. Al- ways so be it. Al- ways so be it.
As we do put our trust in thee. Al- ways so be it. Al- ways so be it.
As we do put our trust in thee. Al- ways so be it. Al- ways so be it.
As we do put our trust in thee. Al- ways so be it. Al- ways so be it.
27
28
29
30
Al- ways so be it. Al- ways so be it. Al- ways so be it. Al- ways so be it.
Al- ways so be it. Al- ways so be it. Al- ways so be it. Al- ways so be it.
Al- ways so be it. Al- ways so be it. Al- ways so be it. Al- ways so be it.
Al- ways so be it. Al- ways so be it. Al- ways so be it. Al- ways so be it.

[2] Te Deum

Triplex
[Contratenor]
Tenor
[Bassus]
We praise thee, O God: we knowl-edge thee to be the Lord.
We praise thee, O God: we knowl-edge thee to be the Lord.
We praise thee, O God: we knowl-edge thee to be the Lord.
We praise thee, O God: we knowl-edge thee to be the Lord.
All the earth might wor-ship thee: which art the Fa-ther ev- er- last-ing. To thee cry forth all
All the earth might wor-ship thee: which art the Fa-ther ev- er- last-ing. To thee cry forth all
All the earth might wor-ship thee: which art the Fa-ther ev- er- last-ing. To thee cry forth all
All the earth might wor-ship thee: which art the Fa-ther ev- er- last-ing. To thee cry forth all
An-gels: the Heav-ens, and all the Powers there-in. To thee thus crieth Cher-u- bin and
An-gels: the Heav-ens, and all the Powers there-in. To thee thus crieth Cher-u- bin and
An-gels: the Heav-ens, and all the Powers there-in. To thee thus crieth Cher-u- bin and
An-gels: the Heav-ens, and all the Powers there-in. To thee thus crieth Cher-u- bin and

20
25
Ser- a- phin: con- tin- u- al- ly, Ho- ly art thou, Ho- ly art thou, Ho- ly art thou:
Ser- a- phin: con- tin- u- al- ly, Ho- ly art thou, Ho- ly art thou, Ho- ly art thou:
Ser- a- phin: con- tin- u- al- ly, Ho- ly art thou, Ho- ly art thou, Ho- ly art thou:
Ser- a- phin: con- tin- u- al- ly, Ho- ly art thou, Ho- ly art thou, Ho- ly art thou:
30
thou art the Lord God of Hosts; Heaven and earth are ful- fill- ed with the Glo- ry
thou art the Lord God of Hosts; Heaven and earth are ful- fill- ed with the Glo- ry
thou art the Lord God of Hosts; Heaven and earth are ful- fill- ed with the Glo- ry
thou art the Lord God of Hosts; Heaven and earth are ful- fill- ed with the Glo- ry
35
of thy Maj-es- ty. The glo- ri-ous com-pa-ny of the A- pos-tles: praise thee. The good-ly
of thy Maj-es- ty. The glo- ri-ous com-pa-ny of the A- pos-tles: praise thee. The good-ly
of thy Maj-es- ty. The glo- ri-ous com-pa-ny of the A-pos- tles: praise thee. The good-ly
of thy Maj-es- ty. The glo- ri-ous com-pa-ny of the A- pos-tles: praise thee. The good-ly
40
45
fel-low-ship of the Pro-phets: wor- ship thee. The fair fel-low-ship of the Mar-tyrs:
fel-low-ship of the Pro-phets: wor-ship thee. The fair fel-low-ship of the Mar-tyrs:
fel-low-ship of the Pro-phets: wor-ship thee. The fair fel-low-ship of the Mar-tyrs:
fel-low-ship of the Pro-phets: wor-ship thee. The fair fel-low-ship of the Mar-tyrs:

50
praise thee. The ho- ly Con- gre- ga- tion of the Faith- ful tho- rough all the
praise thee. The ho- ly Con-gre- ga- tion of the Faith- ful tho- rough all the
praise thee. The ho- ly Con-gre- ga- tion of the Faith- ful tho- rough all the
praise thee. The ho- ly Con-gre- ga- tion of the Faith- ful tho- rough all the
55
world: mag- ni-fy thee. They knowl-edge thee to be the Fa- ther: of an in- fi-
world: mag- ni-fy thee. They knowl-edge thee to be the Fa- ther: of an in- fi-
world: mag- ni-fy thee. They knowl- edge thee to be the Fa- ther: of an in- fi-
world: mag- ni-fy thee. They knowl-edge thee to be the Fa- ther: of an in- fi-
60
- nite Maj- es- ty; They knowl-edge thy hon-our- a- ble and ver- y on- ly Son;
- nite Maj- es- ty; They knowl-edge thy hon- our-a- ble and ver- y on- ly Son;
- nite Maj- es- ty; They knowl-edge thy hon- our-a- ble and ver- y on- ly Son;
- nite Maj- es- ty; They knowl-edge thy hon- our-a- ble and ver- y on- ly Son;
65
they knowl-edge the Ho- ly Ghost to be a Com-for- ter. Thou art King of Glo- ry:
they knowl-edge the Ho- ly Ghost to be a Com-for- ter. Thou art King of Glo- ry:
they knowl-edge the Ho- ly Ghost to be a Com-for- ter. Thou art King of Glo- ry:
they knowl-edge the Ho- ly Ghost to be a Com-for- ter. Thou art King of Glo- ry:

70
O Christ. Thou art the_ev- er- last- ing Son: of the Fa- ther. Thou
O Christ. Thou art the_ev-er- last- ing Son: of the Fa- ther. Thou
O Christ. Thou art the_ev-er- last- ing Son: of the Fa- ther. Thou
O Christ. Thou art the_ev-er- last- ing Son: of the Fa- ther. Thou
75
when thou shouldst take up- on thee our na- ture to de- liv- er man:
when thou shouldst take up- on thee our na- ture to de- liv- er man:
when thou shouldst take up- on thee our na- ture to de- liv- er man:
when thou shouldst take up- on thee our na- ture to de- liv- er man:
80
didst not ab- hor the Vir- gin's womb. Thou hast now o- pened the
didst not ab- hor the Vir- gin's womb. Thou hast now o- pened the
didst not ab- hor the Vir- gin's womb. Thou hast now o- pened the
didst not ab- hor the Vir- gin's womb. Thou hast now o- pened the
85
King- dom of Heav- en to the be- liev- ers: death's dart o- ver- come. Thou
King- dom of Heav- en to the be- liev- ers: death's dart o- ver- come. Thou
King- dom of Heav- en to the be- liev- ers: death's dart o- ver- come. Thou
King- dom of Heav- en to the be- liev- ers: death's dart o- ver- come. Thou

90
sittest on the right hand of God: in the Glo- ry of the Fa- ther. Thou art be-
95
100
- liev- ed to come: our Judge. Where- fore we pray thee, help thy
ser- vants: whom thou hast re- deem- ed with thy pre- cious blood. Make
105
me then num- bered with thy Saints: in joy ev- er- last- ing. O

110
Lord, save thy peo- ple: and bless thine her- i- tage. Gov- ern them
Lord, save thy peo- ple: and bless thine her- i- tage. Gov- ern them
Lord, save thy peo- ple: and bless thine her- i- tage. Gov- ern
Lord, save thy peo- ple: and bless thine her- i- tage. Gov- ern
115
al- so: and lift them up for ev- er. We praise thee ev- e- ry day. And we
al- so: and lift them up for ev- er. We praise thee ev- e- ry day. And we
them al- so: and lift them up for ev- er. We praise thee ev- e- ry day. And we
them al- so: and lift them up for ev- er. We praise thee ev- e- ry day. And we
120
125
wor- ship thy Name: ev- er world with- out end. O Lord, let it
wor- ship thy Name: ev- er world with- out end. O Lord, let it
wor- ship thy Name: ev- er world with- out end. O Lord, let it
wor- ship thy Name: ev- er world with- out end. O Lord, let it
130
be thy pleas-ure: to keep us this day with-out sin. O Lord, have
be thy pleas-ure: to keep us this day with-out sin. O Lord, have
be thy pleas-ure: to keep us this day with-out sin. O Lord, have
be thy pleas-ure: to keep us this day with-out sin. O Lord, have

mer- cy on us: O Lord, have mer- cy on us. O
mer- cy on us: O Lord, have mer- cy on us. O
mer- cy on us: O Lord, have mer- cy on us. O
mer- cy on us: O Lord, have mer- cy on us.
135
Lord, let thy mer- cy light on us: e- ven as we now do
Lord, let thy mer- cy light on us: e- ven as we now do
Lord, let thy mer- cy light on us: e- ven as we now do
O Lord, let thy mer- cy light on us: e- ven as we now do
140
145
trust in thee. O Lord, I trust in thee; I trust in thee: let me
trust in thee. O Lord, I trust in thee; I trust in thee: let me
trust in thee. O Lord, I trust in thee; I trust in thee: let me
trust in thee. O Lord, I trust in thee; I trust in thee: let me
150
nev- er be con- found- ed, let me nev- er be con- found- ed.
nev- er be con- found- ed, let me nev- er be con- found- ed.
nev- er be con- found- ed, let me nev- er be con- found- ed.
nev- er be con- found- ed, let me nev- er be con- found- ed.

[3] De profundis

20
- miss: O Lord, who may a- bide it? For there is mer- cy with thee:
- miss: O Lord, who may a- bide it? For there is mer- cy with thee:
- miss: O Lord, who may a- bide it? For there is mer- cy with thee:
- miss: O Lord, who may a- bide it? For there is mer- cy with thee:
25
there-fore shalt thou be fear-ed. I look for the Lord; my soul doth wait on him:
there-fore shalt thou be fear-ed. I look for the Lord; my soul doth wait on him:
there-fore shalt thou be fear-ed. I look for the Lord; my soul doth wait on him:
there-fore shalt thou be fear-ed. I look for the Lord; my soul doth wait on him:
30
in his word do I trust. My soul fleeth un- to the Lord: be-
in his word do I trust. My soul fleeth un- to the Lord: be-
in his word do I trust. My soul fleeth un- to the Lord: be-
in his word do I trust. My soul fleeth un- to the Lord: be-
35
40
- fore the morn- ing watch, I say, be- fore the morn-ing watch. O Is- ra- el,
- fore the morn- ing watch, I say, be- fore the morn-ing watch. O Is- ra- el,
- fore the morn- ing watch, I say, be- fore the morn-ing watch. O Is- ra- el,
- fore the morn- ing watch, I say, be- fore the morn-ing watch. O Is- ra- el,

45
trust in the Lord, for with the Lord there is mer- cy: and with him is
trust in the Lord, for with the Lord there is mer- cy: and with him is
trust in the Lord, for with the Lord there is mer- cy: and with him is
trust in the Lord, for with the Lord there is mer- cy: and with him is
50
plen- te-ous re- demp- ti- on. And he shall re- deem Is- ra- el: from all his
plen- te- ous re- demp- ti- on. And he shall re- deem Is- ra- el: from all his
plen- te-ous re- demp- ti- on. And he shall re- deem Is- ra- el: from all his
plen- te- ous re- demp- ti- on. And he shall re- deem Is- ra- el: from all his
55
sins. Glo- ry be to the Fa- ther, the Son: and the Ho- ly Ghost;
sins. Glo- ry be to the Fa- ther, the Son: and the Ho- ly Ghost;
sins. Glo- ry be to the Fa- ther, the Son: and the Ho- ly Ghost;
sins. Glo- ry be to the Fa- ther, the Son: and the Ho- ly Ghost;
60
As it was in the be- gin-ning, as it is now, and ev- er shall be: So be it.
As it was in the be- gin-ning, as it is now, and ev- er shall be: So be it.
As it was in the be- gin-ning, as it is now, and ev- er shall be: So be it.
As it was in the be- gin-ning, as it is now, and ev- er shall be: So be it.

[4] Laudate pueri Dominum

25
hea- then: and his glo- ry a- bove the heav- ens. Who is
30
like un- to the Lord our God, that hath his dwell-ing so high: and
35
hum-bleth him-self to be- hold the things that are in heav- en and earth?
40
He takes up the sim- ple out of the dust: and lifts the poor out of the

45
mire; That he may set him with the prin- ces, e- ven with the prin- ces of his
mire; That he may set him with the prin- ces, e- ven with the prin- ces of his
mire; That he may set him with the prin- ces, e- ven with the prin- ces of his
mire; That he may set him with the prin- ces, e- ven with the prin- ces of his
50
peo- ple. He makes the bar- ren wo- man to keep house: and to be a joy- ful
peo- ple. He makes the bar- ren wo- man to keep house: and to be a joy- ful
peo- ple. He makes the bar- ren wo- man to keep house: and to be a joy- ful
peo- ple. He makes the bar- ren wo- man to keep house: and to be a joy- ful
55
mo-ther of chil- dren. Glo-ry be to the Fa- ther, the Son: and the Ho- ly Ghost;
mo-ther of chil- dren. Glo-ry be to the Fa- ther, the Son: and the Ho- ly Ghost;
mo-ther of chil- dren. Glo-ry be to the Fa- ther, the Son: and the Ho- ly Ghost;
mo-ther of chil- dren. Glo-ry be to the Fa- ther, the Son: and the Ho- ly Ghost;
60
As it was in the be- gin-ning, as it is now, and ev- er shall be: So be it.
As it was in the be- gin-ning, as it is now, and ev- er shall be: So be it.
As it was in the be- gin-ning, as it is now, and ev- er shall be: So be it.
As it was in the be- gin-ning, as it is now, and ev- er shall be: So be it.

[5] Ecce quam bonum

20
down to the skirts of his cloth- ing. Like the dew of Her- mon: which
down to the skirts of his cloth- ing. Like the dew of Her- mon: which
down to the skirts of his cloth- ing. Like the dew of Her- mon: which
down to the skirts of his cloth- ing. Like the dew of Her- mon: which
25
fell up- on the hill of Si- on. For there the Lord prom- ised his bless- ing: and
fell up- on the hill of Si- on. For there the Lord prom- ised his bless-ing: and
fell up- on the hill of Si- on. For there the Lord prom- ised his bless- ing: and
fell up- on the hill of Si- on. For there the Lord prom- ised his bless- ing: and
30
al- so life for ev- er-more. Glo- ry be to the Fa- ther, the Son: and the
al- so life for ev- er-more. Glo- ry be to the Fa- ther, the Son: and the
al- so life for ev- er-more. Glo- ry be to the Fa- ther, the Son: and the
al- so life for ev- er-more. Glo- ry be to the Fa- ther, the Son: and the
35
Ho-ly Ghost; As it was in the be-gin-ning, as it is now, and ev- er shall be: So be it.
Ho-ly Ghost; As it was in the be-gin-ning, as it is now, and ev- er shall be: So be it.
Ho-ly Ghost; As it was in the be-gin-ning, as it is now, and ev- er shall be: So be it.
Ho-ly Ghost; As it was in the be-gin-ning, as it is now, and ev- er shall be: So be it.

[6] Iudica me Deus

20
en- my op- press- eth me? O send out thy light and thy truth, that they may
en- my op- press- eth me? O send out thy light and thy truth, that they may
en- my op- press- eth me? O send out thy light and thy truth, that they may
en- my op- press- eth me? O send out thy light and thy truth, that they may
25
lead me: and bring me to thy ho- ly hill, and to thy dwell- ing. And that I may
lead me: and bring me to thy ho- ly hill, and to thy dwell- ing. And that I may
lead me: and bring me to thy ho- ly hill, and to thy dwell- ing. And that I may
lead me: and bring me to thy ho- ly hill, and to thy dwell- ing. And that I may
30
35
go un- to the al- tar of God, even un- to the God of my joy and glad- ness: and up- on the
go un- to the al- tar of God, even un- to the God of my joy and glad- ness: and up- on the
go un- to the al- tar of God, even un- to the God of my joy and glad- ness: and up- on the
go un- to the al- tar of God, even un- to the God of my joy and glad- ness: and up- on the
40
harp will I give thanks to thee, O God, my God. Why art thou so heav- y, O my
harp will I give thanks to thee, O God, my God. Why art thou so heav- y, O my
harp will I give thanks to thee, O God, my God. Why art thou so heav- y, O my
harp will I give thanks to thee, O God, my God. Why art thou so heav- y, O my

45
soul: and why art thou so dis-qui- et- ed with- in me? O put thy trust in God: for I will
soul: and why art thou so dis-qui- et- ed with- in me? O put thy trust in God: for I will
soul: and why art thou so dis-qui- et- ed with- in me? O put thy trust in God: for I will
soul: and why art thou so dis-qui- et- ed with- in me? O put thy trust in God: for I will
50
yet give him thanks, which is the help of my coun- te-nance and my God. Glo- ry
yet give him thanks, which is the help of my coun- te-nance and my God. Glo- ry
yet give him thanks, which is the help of my coun- te-nance and my God. Glo- ry
yet give him thanks, which is the help of my coun- te-nance and my God. Glo- ry
55
be to the Fa- ther, to the Son: and to the Ho- ly Ghost; Even as it
be to the Fa- ther, to the Son: and to the Ho- ly Ghost; Even as it
be to the Fa- ther, to the Son: and to the Ho- ly Ghost; Even as it
be to the Fa- ther, to the Son: and to the Ho- ly Ghost; Even as it
60
was in the be- gin-ning, as it is now, and ev- er shall be: So be it, so be it.
was in the be- gin-ning, as it is now, and ev- er shall be: So be it, so be it.
was in the be- gin-ning, as it is now, and ev- er shall be: So be it, so be it.
was in the be- gin-ning, as it is now, and ev- er shall be: So be it, so be it.

[7] Omnes gentes

20
great King o- ver all the earth, he is the great King o- ver all the earth. He
great King o- ver all the earth, he is the great King o- ver all the earth. He
great King o- ver all the earth, he is the great King o- ver all the earth. He
great King o- ver all the earth, he is the great King o- ver all the earth. He
25
30
shall sub- due the peo-ple un-der us: and the na- ti-ons un- der our feet. He shall choose
shall sub- due the peo-ple un-der us: and the na- ti-ons un- der our feet. He shall choose
shall sub- due the peo-ple un-der us: and the na- ti-ons un- der our feet. He shall choose
shall sub- due the peo-ple un-der us: and the na- ti-ons un- der our feet. He shall choose
35
out an her- i- tage for us, an her- i- tage for us: e- ven the wor- ship of Ja- cob,
out an her- i- tage for us, an her- i- tage for us: e- ven the wor- ship of Ja- cob,
out an her- i- tage for us, an her- i- tage for us: e- ven the wor- ship of Ja- cob,
out an her- i- tage for us, an her- i- tage for us: e- ven the wor- ship of Ja- cob,
e- ven the wor- ship of Ja- cob, whom he lov- ed, whom he lov- ed.
e- ven the wor- ship of Ja- cob, whom he lov- ed, whom he lov- ed.
e- ven the wor- ship of Ja- cob, whom he lov- ed, whom he lov- ed.
e- ven the wor- ship of Ja- cob, whom he lov- ed, whom he lov- ed.

40
God is gone up, God is gone up with a mer- ry noise, with a mer- ry noise: and the
God is gone up, God is gone up with a mer- ry noise, with a mer- ry noise: and the
God is gone up, God is gone up with a mer- ry noise, with a mer- ry noise: and the
God is gone up, God is gone up with a mer- ry noise, with a mer- ry noise: and the
45
Lord, and the Lord with the sound of the trump, and the Lord with the sound of the trump.
Lord, and the Lord with the sound of the trump, and the Lord with the sound of the trump.
Lord, and the Lord with the sound of the trump, and the Lord with the sound of the trump.
Lord, and the Lord with the sound of the trump, and the Lord with the sound of the trump.
50
O sing prais- es, sing prais-es un-to our God: O sing prais- es,
O sing prais- es, sing prais-es un-to our God: O sing prais-
O sing prais- es, sing prais-es un-to our God: O sing prais-
O sing prais- es, sing prais-es un-to our God: O sing prais-
55
sing prais- es to our King, sing prais- es to our King. For
- es, sing prais- es to our King, sing prais- es to our King. For
- es, sing prais- es un- to our King, sing prais- es un- to our King. For
- es, sing prais-es to our King, sing prais- es un- to our King. For

60
God is King of all the earth, of all the earth: Sing prais- es, sing
God is King of all the earth, of all the earth: Sing
God is King of all the earth, of all the earth: Sing prais- es, sing
God is King of all the earth, of all the earth: Sing
65
prais- es with un- der- stand- ing, sing prais- es, sing prais- es with
prais- es with un- der- stand- ing, sing prais- es with
prais- es with un- der- stand- ing, sing prais- es, sing prais- es with
prais- es with un- der- stand- ing, sing prais- es with
70
un- der-stand- ing, with un- der-stand- ing. God reign- eth o- ver the hea- then, God
un- der-stand- ing, with un- der-stand- ing. God reign- eth o- ver the hea- then, God
un- der-stand- ing, with un- der-stand- ing. God reign- eth o- ver the hea- then, God
un- der-stand- ing, with un- der-stand- ing. God reign- eth o- ver the hea- then, God
75
sit- teth up- on his ho- ly seat, his ho- ly seat. The prin- ces of the
sit- teth up- on his ho- ly seat, his ho- ly seat. The prin- ces of the
sit- teth up- on his ho- ly seat, his ho- ly seat. The prin- ces of the
sit- teth up- on his ho- ly seat, his ho- ly seat. The prin- ces of the

80
peo- ple are join- ed to the peo- ple of the God of A- bra- ham, of the
peo- ple are join- ed to the peo- ple of the God of A- bra- ham, of the
peo- ple are join- ed to the peo- ple of the God of A- bra- ham, of the
peo- ple are join- ed to the peo- ple of the God of A- bra- ham, of the
85
God *of A- bra- ham:* for God, which is ver- y high ex- alt- ed, for
God of A- bra- ham: for God, which is ver- y high ex- alt- ed, for
God of A- bra- ham: for God, which is ver- y high ex- alt- ed, for
God of A- bra- ham: for God, which is ver- y high ex- alt- ed, for
90
God, *which is ver- y high* ex- alt- ed, doth de- fend the earth, as it
God, which is ver- y high ex- - alt- ed, doth de- fend the earth, as it
God, *which is ver- y high* ex- alt- ed, doth de- fend the earth, as it
God, which is ver- y high ex- alt- ed, doth de- fend the earth, as it
95
100
were with a shield, *as it were with a shield, as it were with a shield.*
were with a shield, as it were with a shield, as it were with a shield.
were with a shield, as *it were with a shield,* as *it were with a shield.*
were with a shield, as it were with a shield, as it were with a shield.

105
Glo- ry be to the Fa- ther, to the Son: and to the Ho- ly Ghost, and
Glo- ry be to the Fa- ther, to the Son: and to the Ho- ly Ghost, and
Glo- ry be to the Fa- ther, to the Son: and to the Ho- ly Ghost, and
Glo- ry be to the Fa- ther, to the Son: and to the Ho- ly Ghost, and
to the Ho- ly Ghost; Even as it was in the be- gin- ning, as it is
to the Ho- ly Ghost; Even as it was in the be- gin- ning, as it is
to the Ho- ly Ghost; Even as it was in the be- gin- ning, as it is
to the Ho- ly Ghost; Even as it was in the be- gin- ning, as it is
110
115
now, and ev- er shall be, and ev- er shall be: So be it.
now, and ev- er shall be, and ev- er shall be: So be it.
now, and ev- er shall be, and ev- er shall be: So be it.
now, and ev- er shall be, and ev- er shall be: So be it.

[8] Non nobis Domine

15
done what-so-ev-er pleased him. Their i- dols are sil-ver and gold: e- ven the work of men's
done what-so-ev-er pleased him. Their i- dols are sil-ver and gold: e- ven the work of men's
done what-so-ev-er pleased him. Their i- dols are sil-ver and gold: e- ven the work of men's
done what-so-ev-er pleased him. Their i- dols are sil-ver and gold: e- ven the work of men's
20
hands. They have mouths, and speak not: eyes have they, and see not. They have ears, and
hands. They have mouths, and speak not: eyes have they, and see not. They have ears, and
hands. They have mouths, and speak not: eyes have they, and see not. They have ears, and
hands. They have mouths, and speak not: eyes have they, and see not. They have ears, and
25
hear not: no-ses have they, and smell not. They have hands, and han- dle not;
hear not: no-ses have they, and smell not. They have hands, and han- dle not;
hear not: no-ses have they, and smell not. They have hands, and han- dle not;
hear not: no-ses have they, and smell not. They have hands, and han- dle not;
30
feet have they, and walk not: nei- ther speak they through their throat. They that
feet have they, and walk not: nei- ther speak they through their throat. They that
feet have they, and walk not: nei- ther speak they through their throat. They that
feet have they, and walk not: nei- ther speak they through their throat. They that

made them are like un- to them: and so are all they that put their trust in them. But thou,
made them are like un- to them: and so are all they that put their trust in them. But thou,
made them are like un- to them: and so are all they that put their trust in them. But thou,
made them are like un- to them: and so are all they that put their trust in them. But thou,
35
house of Is- ra- el, trust thou in the Lord: he is thy suc- cour and de- fence. Ye
house of Is- ra- el, trust thou in the Lord: he is thy suc- cour and de- fence. Ye
house of Is- ra- el, trust thou in the Lord: he is thy suc- cour and de- fence. Ye
house of Is- ra- el, trust thou in the Lord: he is thy suc- cour and de- fence. Ye
40
house of Aar- on, put your trust in the Lord: he is your help- er and de- fend- er.
house of Aar- on, put your trust in the Lord: he is your help- er and de- fend- er.
house of Aar- on, put your trust in the Lord: he is your help- er and de- fend- er.
house of Aar- on, put your trust in the Lord: he is your help- er and de- fend- er.
45
Ye that fear the Lord, trust ye in the Lord: he is your help- er and de- fend- er.
Ye that fear the Lord, trust ye in the Lord: he is your help- er and de- fend- er.
Ye that fear the Lord, trust ye in the Lord: he is your help- er and de- fend- er.
Ye that fear the Lord, trust ye in the Lord: he is your help- er and de- fend- er.

50
The Lord hath been mind-ful of us, and he shall bless us: e-ven he shall bless the house of
The Lord hath been mind-ful of us, and he shall bless us: e-ven he shall bless the house of
The Lord hath been mind-ful of us, and he shall bless us: e-ven he shall bless the house of
The Lord hath been mind-ful of us, and he shall bless us: e-ven he shall bless the house of
55
Aar-on. He shall bless them that fear the Lord: both great and _ small. The Lord shall in-crease you
Aar-on. He shall bless them that fear the Lord: both great and small. The Lord shall in-crease you
Aar-on. He shall bless them that fear the Lord: both great and _ small. The Lord shall in-crease you
Aar-on. He shall bless them that fear the Lord: both great and small. The Lord shall in-crease you
60
more and more: you and your chil- dren. Ye are the bless- ed of the Lord: which made
more and more: you and your chil- dren. Ye are the bless- ed of the Lord: which made
more and more: you and your chil- dren. Ye are the bless- ed of the Lord: which made
more and more: you and your chil- dren. Ye are the bless- ed of the Lord: which made
65
heav- en and earth. All the whole heav- ens are the Lord's: the earth hath he giv- en
heav- en and earth. All the whole heav- ens are the Lord's: the earth hath he giv- en
heav- en and earth. All the whole heav- ens are the Lord's: the earth hath he giv- en
heav- en and earth. All the whole heav- ens are the Lord's: the earth hath he giv- en

70
un- to the chil- dren of men. The dead praise not thee, O Lord: nei-ther all
75
they that go down to the si- lence. But we will praise the Lord: from this time
80
forth for ev- er- more. Glo- ry be to the Fa- ther, and to the Son: and to the Ho- ly Ghost;
85
E-ven as it was in the be- gin-ning, as it is now, and ev-er shall be: Al-ways so be it.

[9] Deus in nomine tuo

30
eyes, seek af- ter my soul, seek af- ter my soul. He shall re-ward
eyes, seek af- ter my soul, seek af- ter my soul. He shall re-ward
eyes, seek af- ter my soul, seek af- ter my soul. He shall re-ward
eyes, seek af- ter_my soul, seek af- ter my soul. He shall re-ward
35
40
e- vil un- to mine en- mies, un- to mine en- mies; De- stroy them in thy truth, de-
e- vil un- to mine en- mies, un- to mine en- mies; De- stroy them in thy truth, de-
e- vil un- to mine en- mies, un- to mine en- mies; De- stroy them in thy truth, de-
e- vil un- to mine en- mies, un- to mine en- mies; De- stroy them in thy truth, de-
45
- stroy them in thy truth. An of- fering of a free heart will I give
- stroy them in thy truth. An of- fering of a free heart will I give
- stroy them in thy truth. An of- fering of a free heart will I give
- stroy them in thy truth. An of- fering of a free heart will I give
50
55
thee, and praise thy Name, O Lord: be- cause it is so com- fort-a- ble.
thee, and praise thy Name, O Lord: be- cause it is so com- fort-a- ble.
thee, and praise thy Name, O Lord: be- cause it is so com- fort-a- ble.
thee, and praise thy Name, O Lord: be- cause it is so com- fort-a- ble.

60
An of- fering of a free heart will I *give thee, and praise thy*
An of- fering of a free heart will I give thee, and praise thy
An of- fering of a free heart will I give thee, and praise thy
An of- fering of a free heart will I give thee, and praise thy
65
Name, O Lord: be- cause it is so com- fort- a- ble. For he
Name, O Lord: be- cause it is so com- fort- a- ble. For he
Name, O Lord: be- cause it is so com- fort- a- ble. For he
Name, O Lord: be- cause it is so com- fort- a- ble. For he
70
hath de- liv- ered me out from all my trou-ble: [and] mine eye hath
hath de- liv- ered me out from all my trou-ble: and mine eye hath
hath de- liv- ered me out from all my trou- ble: and mine eye hath
hath de- liv- ered me out from all my trou- ble: and mine eye hath
75
80
seen his de- sire up- on mine en- mies, up- on mine en- mies. So be it.
seen his de- sire up- on mine en- mies, up- on mine en- mies. So be it.
seen his de- sire up- on mine en- mies, up- on mine en- mies. So be it.
seen his de- sire up- on mine en- mies, up- on mine en- mies. So be it.

[10] Voce mea

Triplex
Contratenor
Tenor
[Bassus]
5
I cried un- to the Lord with my voice: yea, even un- to the
I cried un- to the Lord with my voice: yea, even un- to the
I cried un- to the Lord with my voice: yea, even un- to the
I cried un- to the Lord with my voice: yea, even un- to the
10
Lord did I make my sup- pli- ca- ti- on. I pour-ed out my com-plaints be-
Lord did I make my sup- pli- ca- ti- on. I pour-ed out my com-plaints be-
Lord did I make my sup- pli- ca- ti- on. I pour-ed out my com-plaints be-
Lord did I make my sup- pli- ca- ti- on. I pour-ed out my com-plaints be-
15
- fore him and showed him of my trou- ble. When my spirit was in heav- i- ness
- fore him and showed him of my trou- ble. When my spirit was in heav- i- ness
- fore him and showed him of my trou- ble. When my spirit was in heav- i- ness
- fore him and showed him of my trou- ble. When my spirit was in heav- i- ness
20
thou knewest my path: in the way where- in I walk-ed have they priv- i- ly
thou knewest my path: in the way where- in I walk-ed have they priv- i- ly
thou knewest my path: in the way where- in I walk-ed have they priv- i- ly
thou knewest my path: in the way where- in I walk-ed have they priv- i- ly

25
laid a snare for me. I look-ed al- so up- on my right_ hand: and see there was
laid a snare for me. I look-ed al- so up- on my right hand: and see there was
laid a snare for me. I look-ed al- so up- on my right hand: and see there was
laid a snare for me. I look-ed al- so up- on my right hand: and see there was
30
no man that would_____ know me. I had no place to flee un- to: and
no man that would know me. I had no place to flee un- to: and
no man that would know me. I had no place to flee un- to: and
no man that would know me. I had no place to flee un- to: and
35
no man car- ed for my soul. I cried un- to thee, O Lord, and said: Thou
no man car- ed for my soul. I cried un- to thee, O Lord, and said: Thou
no man car- ed for my soul. I cried un- to thee, O Lord, and said: Thou
no man car- ed for my soul. I cried un- to thee, O Lord, and said: Thou
40
art my hope, and my por- ti- on in the land of the liv- ing.
art my hope, and my por- ti- on in the land of the liv- ing.
art my hope, and my por- ti- on in the land of the liv- ing.
art my hope, and my por- ti- on in the land of the liv- ing.

45
Con- sid- er my com- plaint: for I am brought ver- y low. O de-
Con- sid- er my com- plaint: for I am brought ver- y low. O de-
Con- sid- er my com- plaint: for I am brought ver- y low. O de-
Con- sid- er my com- plaint: for I am brought ver- y low.
50
- liv- er me from my per- se- cu- tors: for they are too strong for me. Bring my
- liv- er me from my per- se- cu- tors: for they are too strong for me. Bring my
- liv- er me for they are too strong for me. Bring my
from my per- se- cu- tors: for they are too strong for me. Bring my
55
60
soul out of pri- son, that I may give thanks un- to thy Name: which thing if thou wilt
soul out of pri-son, that I may give thanks un- to thy Name: which thing if thou wilt
soul out of pri- son, that I may give thanks un- to thy Name: which thing if thou wilt
soul out of pri- son, that I may give thanks un- to thy Name: which thing if thou wilt
65
grant me, then shall the righ- te-ous re-sort un- to my com-pa- ny. A- men.
grant me, then shall the righ- te-ous re-sort un- to my com- pa-ny. A- men.
grant me, then shall the righ- te-ous re-sort un- to my com- pa-ny. A- men.
grant me, then shall the righ- te-ous re-sort un- to my com- pa-ny. A- men.

[11] Deus misereatur

[Christopher Tye]

15
and bless us, and bless us: and show the light of thy coun- te-nance up-
bless us, and bless us: and show the light of thy coun- te-
us, and bless us, and bless us:
bless us, and bless us:
and show the
20
- on us, up- on us, thy coun- te- nance up- on us,
- nance, of thy coun- te- nance up- on us,
and show the light of thy coun- te-nance up- on us, and show the
light of thy coun- te-nance up- on us, and
and show the light of thy coun- te-nance up-
and show the light of thy coun- te-
light of thy coun- te-nance up- on us,
show the light of thy coun- te-nance up- on us, and show the
25
- on us, up- on us, thy coun-te- nance up- on us; That
- nance, of thy coun- te- nance up- - on us; That we may
and show the light of thy coun- te-nance up- on us;
light of thy coun- te-nance up- on us, up- on us;

30
we may know thy way up- on earth, That we may know
know thy way up- on earth, That we may
That we may know thy way up- on earth,
That we may know thy way up- on earth, may
35
thy way up- - on earth: thy sav- ing health a- mong all the
know thy way up- on earth: thy sav- - ing health a- mong all
thy way up- on earth: thy sav- ing health a- mong all the
know thy way up- on earth: thy sav- ing health a- mong all
40
hea- then, thy sav- ing health a- mong all the hea- then.
hea- then, thy sav- - ing health a- mong all hea- then.
hea- then, thy sav- ing health a- mong all the hea- then.
hea- then, thy sav- ing health a- mong all hea- then.
45
Let the peo- ple praise thee, O God: let all the peo- ple praise thee.
Let the peo- ple praise thee, O God: let all the peo- ple praise thee.
Let the peo- ple praise thee, O God: let all the peo- ple praise thee.
Let the peo- ple praise thee, O God: let all the peo- ple praise thee.

50
O let the peo- ple re- joice and be glad: that thou judg- est them righ- teous-
O let the peo- ple re- joice and be glad: that thou judg- est them righ- teous-
O let the peo- ple re- joice and be glad: that thou judg- est them righ- teous-
O let the peo- ple re- joice and be glad: that thou judg- est them righ- teous-
55
- ly, and gov- ernst all the na- ti- ons up- on the earth, up- on the earth, that
- ly, and gov- ernst all the na- ti- ons up- on the earth, up-
- ly, and gov- ernst all the na- ti- ons that are up-on the
- ly, and gov- ernst all the na- ti- ons up-
60
are up- on the earth, up- on the earth. Let the peo- ple praise thee, O
- on the earth, that are up- on___ the earth. Let the peo- ple praise thee, O
earth, up- on the earth, that are up- on the earth. Let the peo- ple praise thee, O
- on the earth, up- on the earth, up- on the earth. Let the peo- ple praise thee, O

65
God: let all the peo-ple praise thee. God, even our own God, give us thy bless- ing. _
God: let all the peo-ple praise thee. God, even our own God, give us thy bless- ing. _
God: let all the peo-ple praise thee. God, even our own God, give us thy bless-ing.
God: let all the peo-ple praise thee. God, even our own God, give us thy bless-ing.
70
_ That the earth may bring forth all her in- crease: God
_ That the earth may bring forth her in- crease: God
That the earth may bring forth her in- crease, forth her in- crease: God
That the earth may bring forth her in- crease, her _ in- crease: God
75
80
bless us, God bless us, and let all the ends of the world fear him, fear him. So be it, so be it.
bless us, God bless us, and let all the ends of the world fear him, fear him. So be it, so be it.
bless us, God bless us, and let all the ends of the world fear him, fear him. So be it, so be it.
bless us, God bless us, and let all the ends of the world fear him, fear him. So be it, so be it.

[12] Magnificat

20
for he hath looked on the poor de- gree of his ___ hand-maid-en, the poor _
he hath looked on the poor de- gree of his hand- maid- en, the poor de-
of his hand- maid-en, for he hath looked on the poor de- gree of his ___ hand-maid-
- maid- en, for he hath looked on the poor de- gree
25
_ de-gree of his hand- maid- en. Be- hold now, from hence- forth:
- gree of his hand-maid- en, of his hand- maid-en. Be-hold now, from
- en, the poor ______ de- gree of his hand- maid- en. Be-
of his hand-maid- en, of his hand- maid-en. Be-hold
30
35
all gen- er- a- ti-ons shall call me bless- - ed. ______ Be- hold now, from
hence- forth: all gen- er- a- ti-ons shall call me bless- ed. Be-hold
- hold now, from hence- forth: all gen- er- a- ti-ons shall call me bless- ed.
now, from hence- forth: all gen- er- a- ti-ons shall call me bless- ed.
40
hence- forth: all gen- er- a- ti-ons shall call me bless- ed. For
now, from hence- forth: all gen- er- a- ti- ons shall call me bless-
Be- hold now, from hence- forth: all gen- er- a- ti-ons shall
Be- hold now, from hence- forth: all gen- er- a- ti- ons shall call me

45
he that is might- y hath mag-ni- fied me, for he that is
- ed. For he that is might- y hath mag- ni- fied me, for he
call me bless- ed. For he that is might-y hath mag-ni- fied ___ me, ______
bless- ed. For he that is might-y hath mag-ni- fied ______ me,
50
might- y hath mag- ni- fied me, hath mag- ni- fied me: where-
that is might- y hath mag- ni- fied me, mag- ni- fied me: where-
for he that is might- y hath mag- ni- fied me: ______ where-
for he that is might- y hath mag- ni- fied me: where-
55
- fore O bless- ed be his Name, O bless- ed be his Name. And his
- fore O bless- ed be his Name, O bless- ed be his Name. And his
- fore O bless- ed be his Name, O bless- ed be his Name. And his
- fore O bless- ed be his Name, O bless- ed be his Name. And his
60
mer- cy is o- ver them that fear him, that fear him: tho- rough all
mer- cy is o- ver them that fear him, that fear him: tho- rough all
mer- cy is o- ver them that fear him, that fear him: tho- rough all
mer- cy is o- ver them that fear _______ him: tho- rough all

65
gen- er- a- ti- ons. He showeth strength with his arm:
gen- er- a- ti- ons. He showeth strength with his
gen- er- a- ti- ons. He showeth strength with his arm: he
gen- er- a- ti- ons. He showeth strength with his arm: he scat- tereth
he scat- tereth all them that are proud in the i-
arm: he scat- tereth all them that are proud
scat- tereth all them that are proud in the i- ma- gi-
all them that are proud in the i- ma- gi-
70
-ma- gi- na- tion of their hearts. He hath
in the i-ma- gi- na- tion of their hearts. He hath plucked down
-na- tion of their hearts. He hath plucked down men of power
-na- tion of their hearts. He hath plucked down men of power from their
75
plucked down men of power from their seats: and hath lift- - ed up
men of power from their seats: and hath lift- ed up the poor
from their seats: and hath lift- ed up the poor low- ly ones.
seats: and hath lift- ed up the poor low- ly ones.

80
the poor low- ly ones. He hath plucked down men of
low- ly ones. He hath plucked down men of power
— He hath plucked down men of power from their seats:
He hath plucked down men of power from their seats: and hath
85
power from their seats: and hath lift- - ed up the poor low- ly ones. The hun-
from their seats: and hath lift- ed up the poor low- ly ones. The —
and hath lift- ed up, and hath lift- ed up the poor low- ly ones. The hun- gry
lift- ed up, and hath lift- ed up the poor low- ly ones. The
90
- gry men he hath sat- is- fied with — his good- ness, the hun-
— hun- gry men he hath sat- is- fied with his good- ness,
men he hath sat- - is- fied with his — good-ness, the hun- gry
hun- gry men he hath sat- is- fied with his good- ness, the
- gry men he hath sat- is- fied with — his good- ness: and
the hun- gry men he hath sat- is- fied with his good-
men he hath sat- - is- fied with his — good- ness: and them
hun- gry men he hath sat- is- fied with his good- ness:

95
them that ap- pear- ed rich, and them that ap- pear- ed rich he hath left
- ness: and them that ap- pear- ed rich, that ap- pear- ed rich he hath left
that ap-pear-ed rich, and them that ap- pear- ed rich he hath left
and them that ap-pear- ed rich, and them that ap- pear- ed rich he hath left
100
void, he hath left void. He hath tak- en up Is- ra- el his ser- vant:
void, he hath left void. He hath tak- en up Is- ra- el his ser- vant:
void, he hath left void. He hath tak- en up Is- ra- el his ser- vant:
void, he hath left void. He hath tak- en up Is- ra- el his ser- vant:
105
110
think-ing up- on him, think-ing up- on him for to be sav- ed for his
think-ing up- on him, think-ing up- on him for to be sav- ed for his
think-ing up- on him, think-ing up- on him for to be sav- ed for his
think-ing up- on him, think-ing up- on him for to be sav- ed
115
mer-cy's sake, for his mer-cy's sake, his mer- cy's_ sake, Like as he
mer-cy's sake, for his mer- cy's sake, his mer- cy's_ sake, Like as he
mer-cy's sake, for his mer- cy's sake, his mer- cy's sake, Like as he
for his mer- cy's sake, his mer- cy's sake, Like as he

prom- ised to our fa- thers, as to A- bra- ham,
prom- ised to our fa- thers, as to A- bra- ham, as
prom- ised to our fa- thers, as to A- bra-ham, as to
prom- ised to our fa- thers, our fa- thers, as to A- bra-
120
as to A- bra- ham and to his seed for ev- er-
to A- bra- ham and to his seed, and to his seed for
A- bra-ham and to his seed for ev- er-more, and
-ham and to his seed for ev- er- more, and
125
-more, and to his seed for ev- er- more. Glo- ry be to the
ev- er-more, and to his seed for ev- er-more. Glo- ry be to the
to his seed for ev- er-more, for ev- er-more. Glo- ry be to the
to his seed for ev- er- more. Glo- ry be to the
130
Fa- ther, to the Son: and to the Ho- ly Ghost; E-ven as it
Fa- ther, to the Son: and to the Ho- ly Ghost; E-ven
Fa- ther, to the Son: and to the Ho- ly Ghost;
Fa- ther, to the Son: and to the Ho- ly Ghost;

135
was in the be- gin- ning, ev-en as it was in the be-gin- ning, as it is now,
as it was in the be- gin- ning, e-ven as it was in the be- gin- ning, as it is now, as
E-ven as it was in the be- gin- ning, as it is now, as
E- ven as it was in the be-gin- ning, as
140
and ev- er shall be: as it is now, and ev- er shall be:
it is now, and ev- er shall be: so be it, and ev- er shall
it is now, and ev- er, and ev- er shall be, ev- er shall be,
it is now, and ev- er shall be, ev- er shall be: so be it,
145
so be it, and ev- er shall be, Al- ways so be it, so be it.
be: so be it, and ev- er shall be, Al- ways so be it, so be it.
and ev- er shall be: so be it, Al- ways so be it, so be it.
and ev- er shall be, Al- ways so be it, so be it.

[13] Ne reminiscaris

[Thomas Tallis]

20
Sav- i- our, And for the glory of thy Name de- liv- er
Sav- i- our, And for the glo- ry of thy Name de- liv- er
Sav- i- our, And for the glo- ry of thy Name de- - liv- er
Sav- i- our, And for the glo- ry of thy Name de- liv- er
25
us, be mer- ci- ful and for- give us our sins, for
us, be mer- ci- ful and for- give us our sins, for
us, be mer- ci- ful and for- give us our sins, for
us, be mer- ci- ful and for- give us our sins, for
30
thy Name's sake. Let not the wick- ed peo- ple say: Where is
thy Name's sake. Let not the wick- ed peo- ple say: Where is
thy Name's sake. Let not the wick- ed peo- ple say: Where is
thy Name's sake. Let not the wick- ed peo- ple say: Where is
35
their God? We be thy peo- ple and the sheep of thy pas- ture,
their God? We be thy peo- ple and the sheep of thy pas- ture,
their God? We be thy peo- ple and the sheep of thy pas- ture,
their God? We be thy peo- ple and the sheep of thy pas- ture,

40
we shall give thanks un- to thee for ev- er: from age to age
we shall give thanks un- to thee for ev- er: from age to age
we shall give thanks un- to thee for ev- er: from age to age
we shall give thanks un- to thee for ev- er: from age to age
45
we shall set forth thy laud and praise. To thee be hon- our and
we shall set forth thy laud and praise. To thee be hon- our and
we shall set forth thy laud and praise. To thee be hon- our and
we shall set forth thy laud and praise. To thee be hon- our and
50
glo- ry, world with- out end, world with- out end. So be it.
glo- ry, world with- out end, world with- out end. So be it.
glo- ry, world with- out end, world with- out end. So be it.
glo- ry, world with- out end, world with- out end. So be it.

[14] Iubilate Deo

15
sprite, one God ______ a- lone. Con- fess, ___ con- fess his maj- es- ty, ______ one
us, con-fess ______ we must. His peo- ple in- deed a flock we are, ______ whom
-bly in ev- - ery place. Speak, read ___ and ___ sing his laud and praise, ___ his
-ty and the ______ ful- ness. His prom- i- ses be most con-stant sure, ______ in
might, in per- - sons three. Even as _____ it _____ was in the be- gin- ning, and
sprite, one God a- lone. Con- fess, ___ con- fess his maj- es- ty, ______ one
us, con- fess we must. His peo- ple in- deed a flock we are, ______ whom
-bly in ev- ery place. Speak, read ___ and ___ sing his laud and praise, ___ his
-ty and the ful- ness. His prom- i- ses be most con-stant sure, ______ in
might, in per- sons three. Even as _____ it _____ was in the be- gin- ning, and
sprite, one God a- lone. Con- fess, ___ con- fess his maj- es- ty, ______ one
us, con- fess we must. His peo- ple in- deed a flock we are, ______ whom
-bly in ev- ery place. Speak, read ___ and ___ sing his laud and praise, ___ his
-ty and the ful- ness. His prom- i- ses be most con-stant sure, ______ in
might, in per- sons three. Even as _____ it _____ was in the be- gin- ning, and
sprite, one God a- lone. Con- fess, ___ con- fess his maj- es- ty, ______ one
us, con- fess we must. His peo- ple in- deed a flock we are, ______ whom
-bly in ev- ery place. Speak, read ___ and ___ sing his laud and praise, ___ his
-ty and the ful- ness. His prom- i- ses be most con-stant sure, ______ in
might, in per- sons three. Even as _____ it _____ was in the be- gin- ning, and
20
God doubt- less in Trin- i- ty, one God doubt- less in Trin- i- ty.
he doth feed with bus- y care, whom he doth feed with bus- y care.]
glad tid- ing, his word al- ways, his glad tid- ing, his word al- ways. So be it.
each de- gree, al- ways to en-dure, in each de- gree, al- ways to en-dure.]
shall be, time with- out end- ing, and shall be, time with- out end- ing.]
God doubt- less in Trin- i- ty, one God doubt- less in Trin- - i- ty.
he doth feed with bus- y care, whom he doth feed with bus- - y care.
glad tid- ing, his word al- ways, his glad tid- ing, his word ____ al- ways. So be it.
each de- gree, al- ways to en-dure, in each de- gree, al- ways ____ to en- dure.
shall be, time with- out end- ing, and shall be, time with- out ____ end- ing.
God doubt- less in Trin- i- ty, one God doubt- less in Trin- i- ty.
he doth feed with bus- y care, whom he doth feed with bus- y care.
glad tid- ing, his word al- ways, his glad tid- ing, his word al- ways. So be it.
each de- gree, al- ways to en-dure, in each de- gree, al- ways to en- dure.
shall be, time with- out end- ing, and shall be, time with- out end- ing.
God doubt- less in Trin- i- ty, one God doubt- less in Trin- i- ty.
he doth feed with bus- y care, whom he doth feed with bus- y care.
glad tid- ing, his word al- ways, his glad tid- ing, his word al- ways. So be it.
each de- gree, al- ways to en-dure, in each de- gree, al- ways to en- dure.
shall be, time with- out end- ing, and shall be, time with- out end- ing.

[15] Benedicite

30
praise him, all Powers both great and small, all Spirits and Bod-ies as ye are bound: in one con-sent praise
praise him, all Powers both great and small, all Spirits and Bod-ies as ye are bound: in one con-sent praise
praise him, all Powers both great and small, all Spirits and Bod-ies as ye are bound: in one con-sent praise
35
him to-geth-er, ex- tol and laud ye him for ev- er. O praise the Lord.
him to-geth-er, ex- tol and laud ye him for ev- er. O praise the Lord.
him to-geth-er, ex- tol and laud ye him for ev- er. O praise the Lord.
CHOIR I, II
40
[2.]Praise the Lord. Ye An- gels and ye Heav- ens a- bove, ye
[3.]Praise the Lord. Ye Rains, ye Dews, ye bois- terous Winds, O
[4.]Praise the Lord. Thou Earth with Hills and Moun- tains high, all
[5.]Praise the Lord. Look up, Is- ra- el, with joy- ful cheer, and
[6.]Praise the Lord. A- na- nye, A- za-rye, Mi- sa- el,
[2.]Praise the Lord. Ye An- gels and ye Heav- ens a- bove, ye
[3.]Praise the Lord. Ye Rains, ye Dews, ye bois- terous Winds, O
[4.]Praise the Lord. Thou Earth with Hills and Moun- tains high, all
[5.]Praise the Lord. Look up, Is- ra- el, with joy- ful cheer, and
[6.]Praise the Lord. A- na- nye, A- za-rye, Mi- sa- el,
[2.]Praise the Lord. Ye An- gels and ye Heav- ens a- bove, ye
[3.]Praise the Lord. Ye Rains, ye Dews, ye bois- terous Winds, O
[4.]Praise the Lord. Thou Earth with Hills and Moun- tains high, all
[5.]Praise the Lord. Look up, Is- ra- el, with joy- ful cheer, and
[6.]Praise the Lord. A- na- nye, A- za-rye, Mi- sa- el,

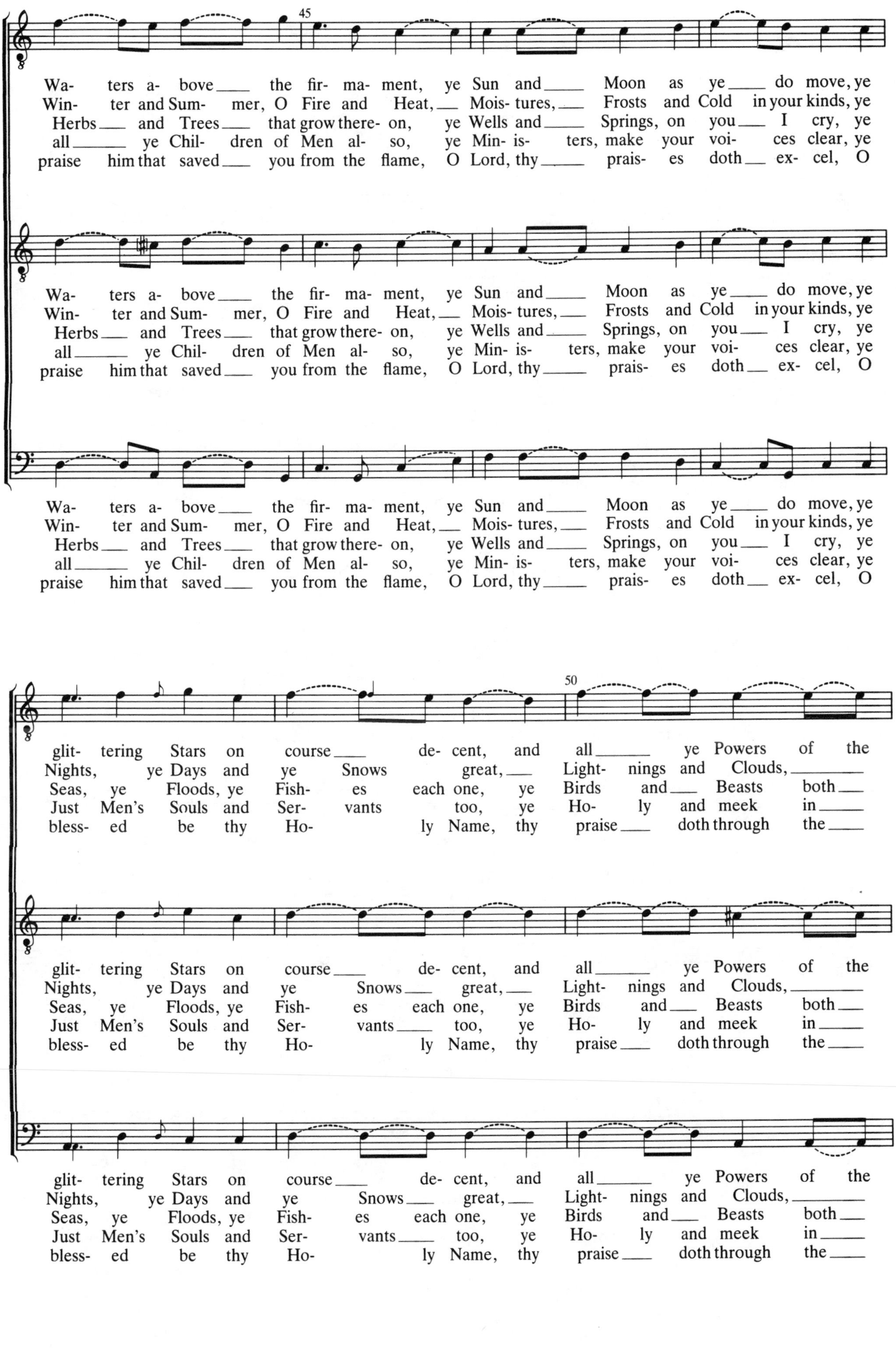
45
Wa- ters a- bove ___ the fir- ma- ment, ye Sun and ___ Moon as ye ___ do move, ye
Win- ter and Sum- mer, O Fire and Heat, __ Mois- tures, __ Frosts and Cold in your kinds, ye
Herbs ___ and Trees ___ that grow there- on, ye Wells and ___ Springs, on you ___ I cry, ye
all ___ ye Chil- dren of Men al- so, ye Min- is- ters, make your voi- ces clear, ye
praise him that saved ___ you from the flame, O Lord, thy ___ prais- es doth ___ ex- cel, O
Wa- ters a- bove ___ the fir- ma- ment, ye Sun and ___ Moon as ye ___ do move, ye
Win- ter and Sum- mer, O Fire and Heat, __ Mois- tures, __ Frosts and Cold in your kinds, ye
Herbs ___ and Trees ___ that grow there- on, ye Wells and ___ Springs, on you ___ I cry, ye
all ___ ye Chil- dren of Men al- so, ye Min- is- ters, make your voi- ces clear, ye
praise him that saved ___ you from the flame, O Lord, thy ___ prais- es doth ___ ex- cel, O
Wa- ters a- bove ___ the fir- ma- ment, ye Sun and ___ Moon as ye ___ do move, ye
Win- ter and Sum- mer, O Fire and Heat, __ Mois- tures, __ Frosts and Cold in your kinds, ye
Herbs ___ and Trees ___ that grow there- on, ye Wells and ___ Springs, on you ___ I cry, ye
all ___ ye Chil- dren of Men al- so, ye Min- is- ters, make your voi- ces clear, ye
praise him that saved ___ you from the flame, O Lord, thy ___ prais- es doth ___ ex- cel, O
50
glit- tering Stars on course ___ de- cent, and all ___ ye Powers of the
Nights, ye Days and ye Snows great, ___ Light- nings and Clouds, ___
Seas, ye Floods, ye Fish- es each one, ye Birds and ___ Beasts both ___
Just Men's Souls and Ser- vants too, ye Ho- ly and meek in ___
bless- ed be thy Ho- ly Name, thy praise ___ doth through the ___
glit- tering Stars on course ___ de- cent, and all ___ ye Powers of the
Nights, ye Days and ye Snows ___ great, ___ Light- nings and Clouds, ___
Seas, ye Floods, ye Fish- es each one, ye Birds and ___ Beasts both ___
Just Men's Souls and Ser- vants ___ too, ye Ho- ly and meek in ___
bless- ed be thy Ho- ly Name, thy praise ___ doth through the ___
glit- tering Stars on course ___ de- cent, and all ___ ye Powers of the
Nights, ye Days and ye Snows ___ great, ___ Light- nings and Clouds, ___
Seas, ye Floods, ye Fish- es each one, ye Birds and ___ Beasts both ___
Just Men's Souls and Ser- vants ___ too, ye Ho- ly and meek in ___
bless- ed be thy Ho- ly Name, thy praise ___ doth through the ___

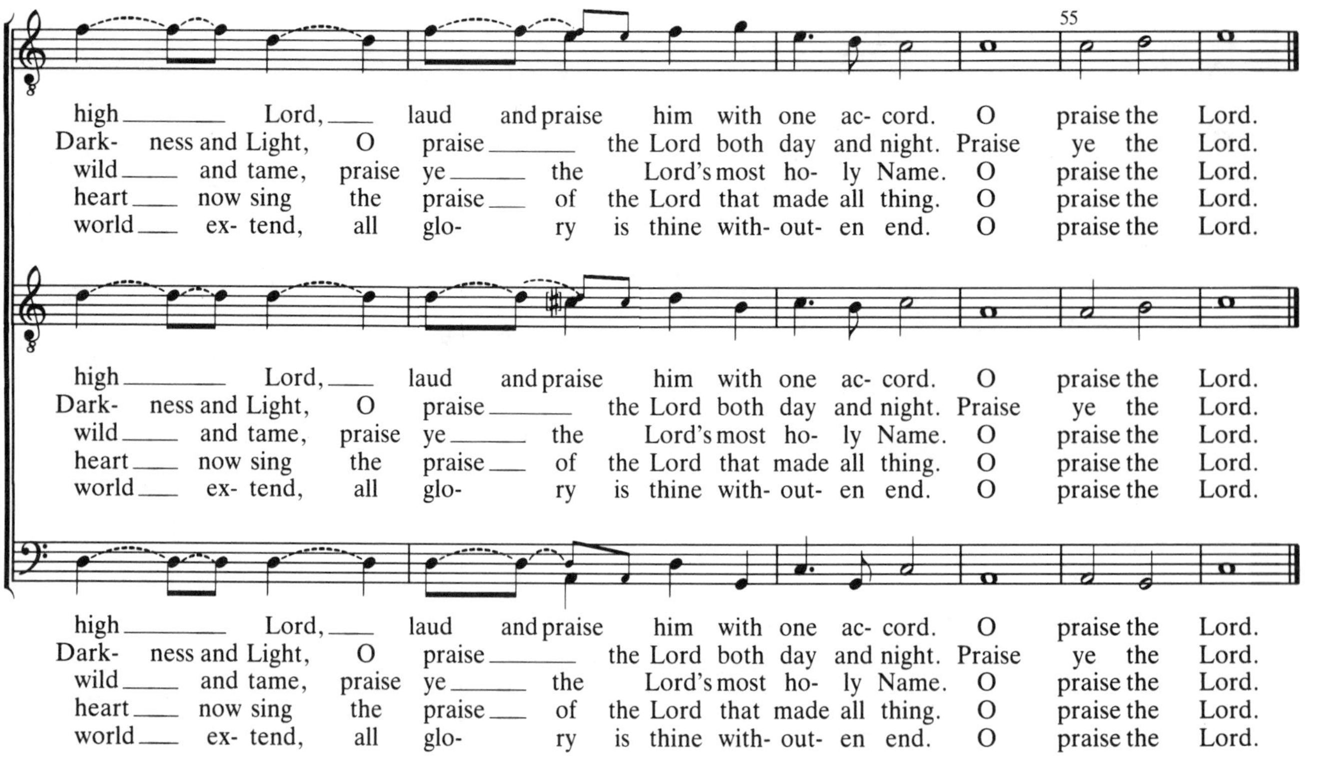
55
high Lord, laud and praise him with one ac- cord. O praise the Lord.
Dark- ness and Light, O praise the Lord both day and night. Praise ye the Lord.
wild and tame, praise ye the Lord's most ho- ly Name. O praise the Lord.
heart now sing the praise of the Lord that made all thing. O praise the Lord.
world ex- tend, all glo- ry is thine with- out- en end. O praise the Lord.
high Lord, laud and praise him with one ac- cord. O praise the Lord.
Dark- ness and Light, O praise the Lord both day and night. Praise ye the Lord.
wild and tame, praise ye the Lord's most ho- ly Name. O praise the Lord.
heart now sing the praise of the Lord that made all thing. O praise the Lord.
world ex- tend, all glo- ry is thine with- out- en end. O praise the Lord.
high Lord, laud and praise him with one ac- cord. O praise the Lord.
Dark- ness and Light, O praise the Lord both day and night. Praise ye the Lord.
wild and tame, praise ye the Lord's most ho- ly Name. O praise the Lord.
heart now sing the praise of the Lord that made all thing. O praise the Lord.
world ex- tend, all glo- ry is thine with- out- en end. O praise the Lord.

[16] Benedictus

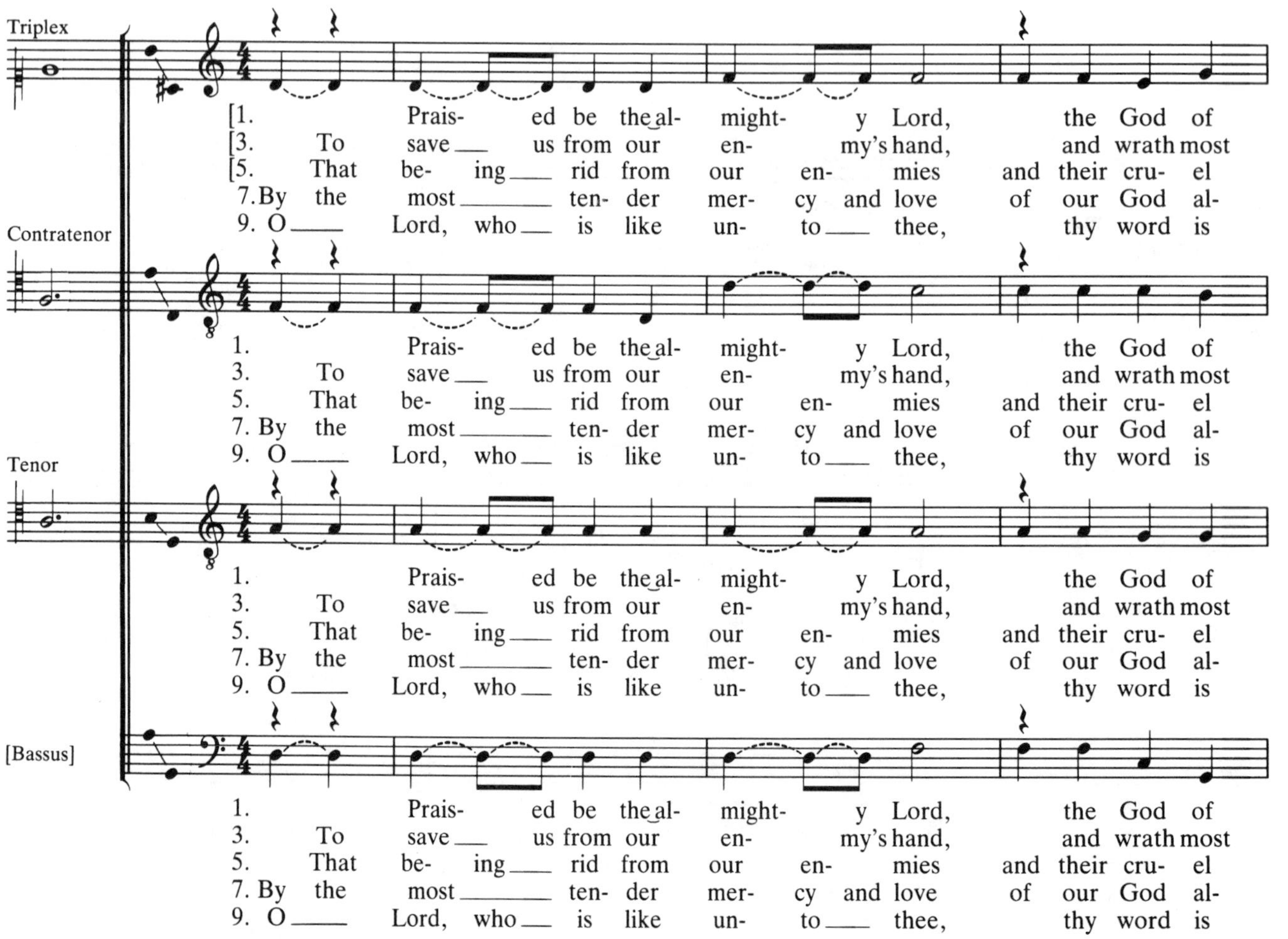
Triplex
[1. Prais- ed be the al- might- y Lord, the God of
[3. To save us from our en- my's hand, and wrath most
[5. That be- ing rid from our en- mies and their cru- el
7. By the most ten- der mer- cy and love of our God al-
9. O Lord, who is like un- to thee, thy word is
Contratenor
1. Prais- ed be the al- might- y Lord, the God of
3. To save us from our en- my's hand, and wrath most
5. That be- ing rid from our en- mies and their cru- el
7. By the most ten- der mer- cy and love of our God al-
9. O Lord, who is like un- to thee, thy word is
Tenor
1. Prais- ed be the al- might- y Lord, the God of
3. To save us from our en- my's hand, and wrath most
5. That be- ing rid from our en- mies and their cru- el
7. By the most ten- der mer- cy and love of our God al-
9. O Lord, who is like un- to thee, thy word is
[Bassus]
1. Prais- ed be the al- might- y Lord, the God of
3. To save us from our en- my's hand, and wrath most
5. That be- ing rid from our en- mies and their cru- el
7. By the most ten- der mer- cy and love of our God al-
9. O Lord, who is like un- to thee, thy word is

Is- ra- el, that hath ac- cord- ing to__ his word dealt
fur- i- ous, and al- so__ from the cru- el band of
bold- ness, we might free- ly do him ser- vice in
- might- y, where- by he,__ com- ing from a- bove, did
ev- er__ pure, thy prom- is- es most__ con- stant__ be, and
Is- ra- el, that hath ac- cord- ing to__ his word dealt
fur- i- ous, and al- so__ from the cru- el band of
bold- ness, we might free- ly do him ser- vice in
- might- y, where- by he,__ com- ing from a- bove, did
ev- er__ pure, thy prom- is- es most__ con- stant__ be, and
Is- ra- el, that hath ac- cord- ing to his__ word dealt
fur- i- ous, and al- so__ from the__ cru- el band of
bold- ness, we might free- ly do__ him ser- vice in
- might- y, where- by he,__ com- ing from a- bove, did
ev- er__ pure, thy prom- is- es most__ con- stant__ be, and
Is- ra- el, that hath ac- cord- ing to his__ word dealt
fur- i- ous, and al- so__ from the__ cru- el band of
bold- ness, we might free- ly do__ him ser- vice in
- might- y, where- by he,__ com- ing__ from a- bove, did
ev- er__ pure, thy prom- is- es most__ con- stant__ be, and
with his peo- ple well, to vis- it them as he hath done, per-
all that hat- ed us, to show our__ fa- thers his mer- cy, as
right and ho- li- ness, be- fore__ his pres- ence with all praise, in
vis- it us free- ly, to light- en them that, com- fort- less, sat
al- ways so en- dure, all glo- ry, praise and all hon- our is
with his peo- ple well, to vis- it them as he hath done, per-
all that hat- ed us, to show our__ fa- thers his mer- cy, as
right and ho- li- ness, be- fore__ his pres- ence with all praise, in
vis- it us free- ly, to light- en them that, com- fort- less, sat
al- ways so en- dure, all glo- ry, praise and all hon- our is
with his peo- ple well, to vis- it them as he hath done, per-
all that hat- ted us, to show our fa- thers his mer- cy, as
right and ho- li- ness, be- fore his pres- ence with all praise, in
vis- it us free- ly, to light- en them that, com- fort- less, sat
al- ways so en- dure, all glo- ry, praise and all hon- our is
with his peo- ple well, to vis- it them as he hath done, per-
all that hat- ed us, to show our fa- thers his mer- cy, as
right and ho- li- ness, be- fore his pres- ence with all praise, in
vis- it us free- ly, to light- en them that, com- fort- less, sat
al- ways so en- dure, all glo- ry, praise and all hon- our is

15
-form- ing their re- demp- ti- on, per- form- ing their re- demp- ti- on.]
he prom- ised most faith- ful- ly, as he prom- ised most faith- ful- ly.]
spirit and truth all our life days, in spirit and truth all our life days.]
in the foul fog of dark- ness, sat in the foul fog of dark- ness.
thine, O Lord, for ev- er- more, is thine, O Lord, for ev- er- more.
-form- ing their re- demp- ti- on, per- form- ing their re- demp- ti- on.
he prom- ised most faith- ful- ly, as he prom- ised most faith- ful- ly.
spirit and truth all our life days, in spirit and truth all our life days.
in the foul fog of dark- ness, sat in the foul fog of dark- ness.
thine, O Lord, for ev- er- more, is thine, O Lord, for ev- er- more.
-form- ing their re- demp- ti- on, per- form- ing their re- demp- ti- on.
he prom- ised most faith- ful- ly, as he prom- ised most faith- ful- ly.
spirit and truth all our life days, in spirit and truth all our life days.
in the foul fog of dark- ness, sat in the foul fog of dark- ness.
thine, O Lord, for ev- er- more, is thine, O Lord, for ev- er- more.
-form- ing their re- demp- ti- on, per- form- ing their re- demp- ti- on.
he prom- ised most faith- ful- ly, as he prom- ised most faith- ful- ly.
spirit and truth all our life days, in spirit and truth all our life days.
in the foul fog of dark- ness, sat in the foul fog of dark- ness.
thine, O Lord, for ev- er- more, is thine, O Lord, for ev- er- more.
20
2. A sav- ing health vic- to- ri- ous he hath sent us tru- ly,
4. His ho- ly test- ment to de- clare as the time prom- ised came,
6. And thou, child, shalt the pro- phet hight of him that is most high,
8. To light- en those that in the shade of death did sit al- so,
2. A sav- ing health vic- to- ri- ous he hath sent us tru- ly,
4. His ho- ly test- ment to de- clare as the time prom- ised came,
6. And thou, child, shalt the pro- phet hight of him that is most high,
8. To light- en those that in the shade of death did sit al- so,
2. A sav- ing health vic- to- ri- ous he hath sent us tru- ly,
4. His ho- ly test- ment to de- clare as the time prom- ised came,
6. And thou, child, shalt the pro- phet hight of him that is most high,
8. To light- en those that in the shade of death did sit al- so,
2. A sav- ing health vic- to- ri- ous he hath sent us tru- ly,
4. His ho- ly test- ment to de- clare as the time prom- ised came,
6. And thou, child, shalt the pro- phet hight of him that is most high,
8. To light- en those that in the shade of death did sit al- so,

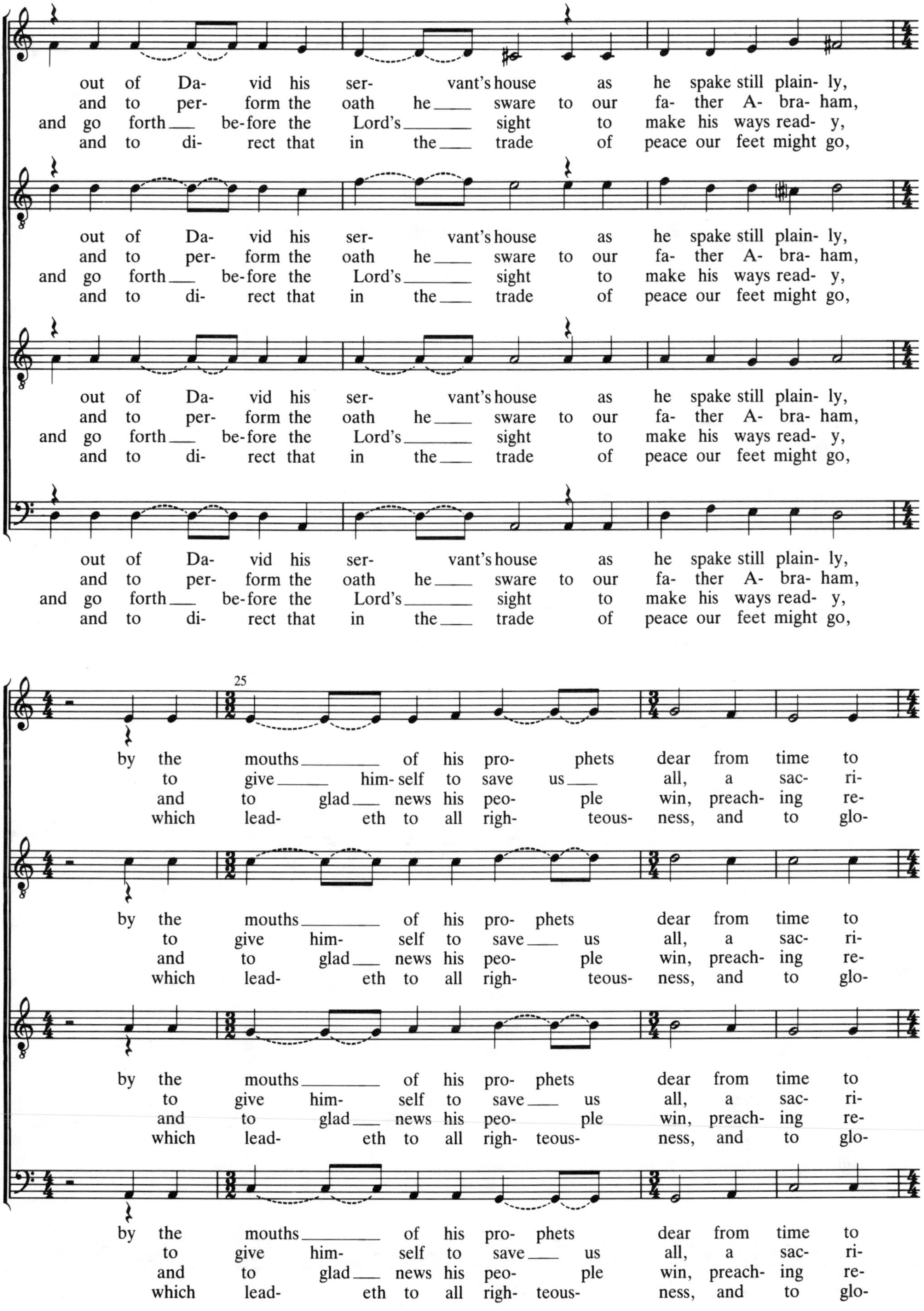
out of Da- vid his ser- vant's house as he spake still plain- ly,
and to per- form the oath he sware to our fa- ther A- bra- ham,
and go forth before the Lord's sight to make his ways read- y,
and to di- rect that in the trade of peace our feet might go,
out of Da- vid his ser- vant's house as he spake still plain- ly,
and to per- form the oath he sware to our fa- ther A- bra- ham,
and go forth before the Lord's sight to make his ways read- y,
and to di- rect that in the trade of peace our feet might go,
out of Da- vid his ser- vant's house as he spake still plain- ly,
and to per- form the oath he sware to our fa- ther A- bra- ham,
and go forth before the Lord's sight to make his ways read- y,
and to di- rect that in the trade of peace our feet might go,
out of Da- vid his ser- vant's house as he spake still plain- ly,
and to per- form the oath he sware to our fa- ther A- bra- ham,
and go forth before the Lord's sight to make his ways read- y,
and to di- rect that in the trade of peace our feet might go,
25
by the mouths of his pro- phets dear from time to
to give him- self to save us all, a sac- ri-
and to glad news his peo- ple win, preach- ing re-
which lead- eth to all righ- teous- ness, and to glo-
by the mouths of his pro- phets dear from time to
to give him- self to save us all, a sac- ri-
and to glad news his peo- ple win, preach- ing re-
which lead- eth to all righ- teous- ness, and to glo-
by the mouths of his pro- phets dear from time to
to give him- self to save us all, a sac- ri-
and to glad news his peo- ple win, preach- ing re-
which lead- eth to all righ- teous- ness, and to glo-
by the mouths of his pro- phets dear from time to
to give him- self to save us all, a sac- ri-
and to glad news his peo- ple win, preach- ing re-
which lead- eth to all righ- teous- ness, and to glo-

30
time that ev- er were, from time to time that ev- er were.
-fice per- pet- u- al, a sac- ri- fice per- pet- u- al.
-mis- sion of their sin, preach- ing re- mis- sion of their sin.
-ry that is end- less, and to glo- ry that is end- less.
time that ev- er were, from time to time that ev- er were.
-fice per- pet- u- al, a sac- ri- fice per- pet- u- al.
-mis- sion of their sin, preach- ing re- mis- sion of their sin.
-ry that is end- less, and to glo- ry that is end- less.
time that ev- er were, from time to time that ev- er were.
-fice per- pet- u- al, a sac- ri- fice per- pet- u- al.
-mis- sion of their sin, preach- ing re- mis- sion of their sin.
-ry that is end- less, and to glo- ry that is end- less.
time that ev- er were, from time to time that ev- er were.
-fice per- pet- u- al, a sac- ri- fice per- pet- u- al.
-mis- sion of their sin, preach- ing re- mis- sion of their sin.
-ry that is end- less, and to glo- ry that is end- less.
35
40
10. All glo- ry, praise and all hon- our is thine, O Lord, for ev- er- more. So be it.
[10.] All glo- ry, praise and all hon- our is thine, O Lord, for ev- er- more. So be it.
[10.] All glo- ry, praise and all hon- our is thine, O Lord, for ev- er- more. So be it.
10. All glo- ry, praise and all hon- our is thine, O Lord, for ev- er- more. So be it.

[17] Domine Dominus noster

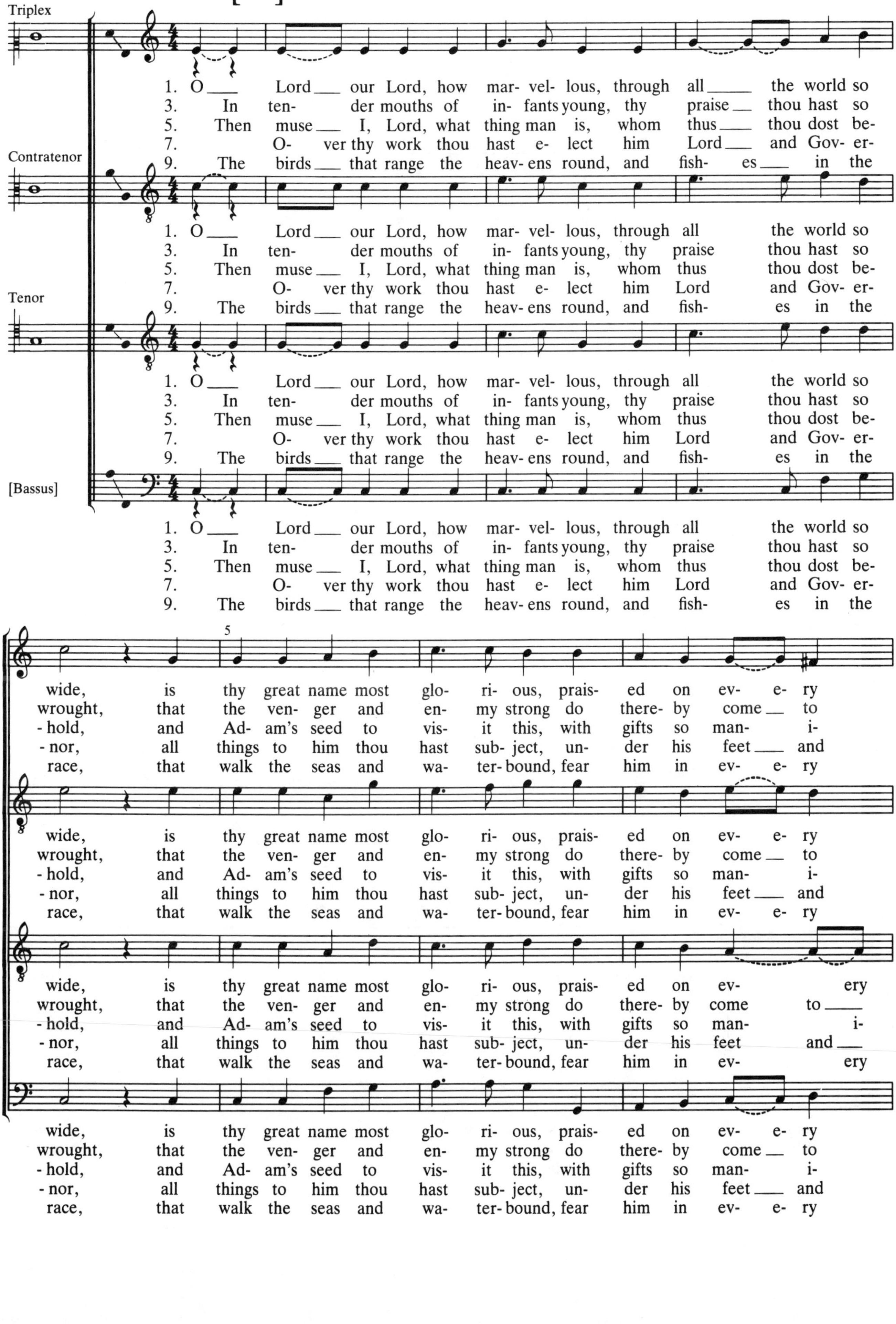

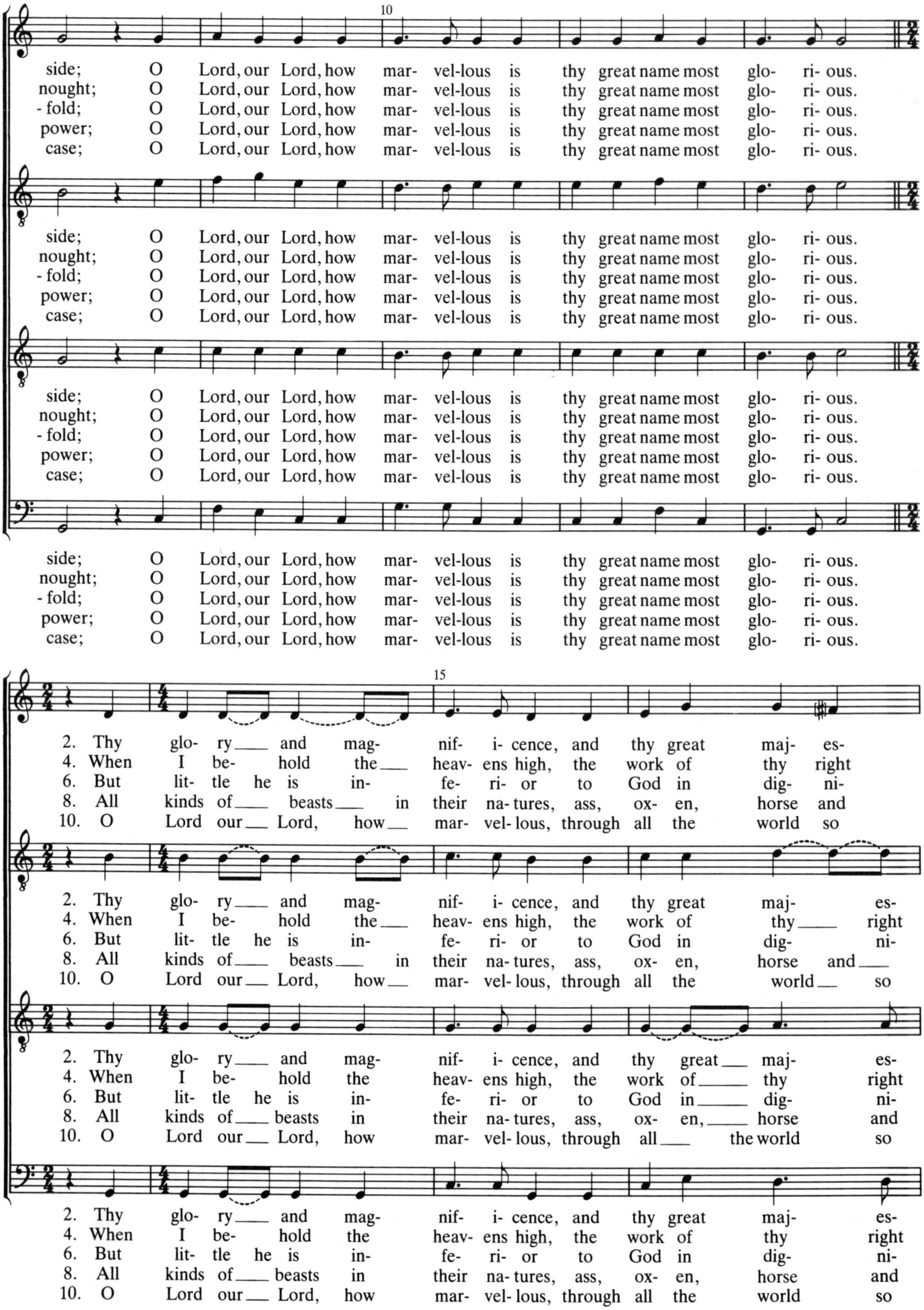
10
side; O Lord, our Lord, how mar- vel-lous is thy great name most glo- ri- ous.
nought; O Lord, our Lord, how mar- vel-lous is thy great name most glo- ri- ous.
- fold; O Lord, our Lord, how mar- vel-lous is thy great name most glo- ri- ous.
power; O Lord, our Lord, how mar- vel-lous is thy great name most glo- ri- ous.
case; O Lord, our Lord, how mar- vel-lous is thy great name most glo- ri- ous.
side; O Lord, our Lord, how mar- vel-lous is thy great name most glo- ri- ous.
nought; O Lord, our Lord, how mar- vel-lous is thy great name most glo- ri- ous.
- fold; O Lord, our Lord, how mar- vel-lous is thy great name most glo- ri- ous.
power; O Lord, our Lord, how mar- vel-lous is thy great name most glo- ri- ous.
case; O Lord, our Lord, how mar- vel-lous is thy great name most glo- ri- ous.
side; O Lord, our Lord, how mar- vel-lous is thy great name most glo- ri- ous.
nought; O Lord, our Lord, how mar- vel-lous is thy great name most glo- ri- ous.
- fold; O Lord, our Lord, how mar- vel-lous is thy great name most glo- ri- ous.
power; O Lord, our Lord, how mar- vel-lous is thy great name most glo- ri- ous.
case; O Lord, our Lord, how mar- vel-lous is thy great name most glo- ri- ous.
side; O Lord, our Lord, how mar- vel-lous is thy great name most glo- ri- ous.
nought; O Lord, our Lord, how mar- vel-lous is thy great name most glo- ri- ous.
- fold; O Lord, our Lord, how mar- vel-lous is thy great name most glo- ri- ous.
power; O Lord, our Lord, how mar- vel-lous is thy great name most glo- ri- ous.
case; O Lord, our Lord, how mar- vel-lous is thy great name most glo- ri- ous.
15
2. Thy glo- ry___ and mag- nif- i- cence, and thy great maj- es-
4. When I be- hold the___ heav- ens high, the work of thy right
6. But lit- tle he is in- fe- ri- or to God in dig- ni-
8. All kinds of___ beasts___ in their na- tures, ass, ox- en, horse and
10. O Lord our___ Lord, how___ mar- vel- lous, through all the world so
2. Thy glo- ry___ and mag- nif- i- cence, and thy great maj- es-
4. When I be- hold the___ heav- ens high, the work of thy___ right
6. But lit- tle he is in- fe- ri- or to God in dig- ni-
8. All kinds of___ beasts___ in their na- tures, ass, ox- en, horse and___
10. O Lord our___ Lord, how___ mar- vel- lous, through all the world___ so
2. Thy glo- ry___ and mag- nif- i- cence, and thy great___ maj- es-
4. When I be- hold the heav- ens high, the work of___ thy right
6. But lit- tle he is in- fe- ri- or to God in___ dig- ni-
8. All kinds of___ beasts in their na- tures, ass, ox- en,___ horse and
10. O Lord our___ Lord, how mar- vel- lous, through all___ the world so
2. Thy glo- ry___ and mag- nif- i- cence, and thy great maj- es-
4. When I be- hold the heav- ens high, the work of thy right
6. But lit- tle he is in- fe- ri- or to God in dig- ni-
8. All kinds of___ beasts in their na- tures, ass, ox- en, horse and
10. O Lord our___ Lord, how mar- vel- lous, through all the world so

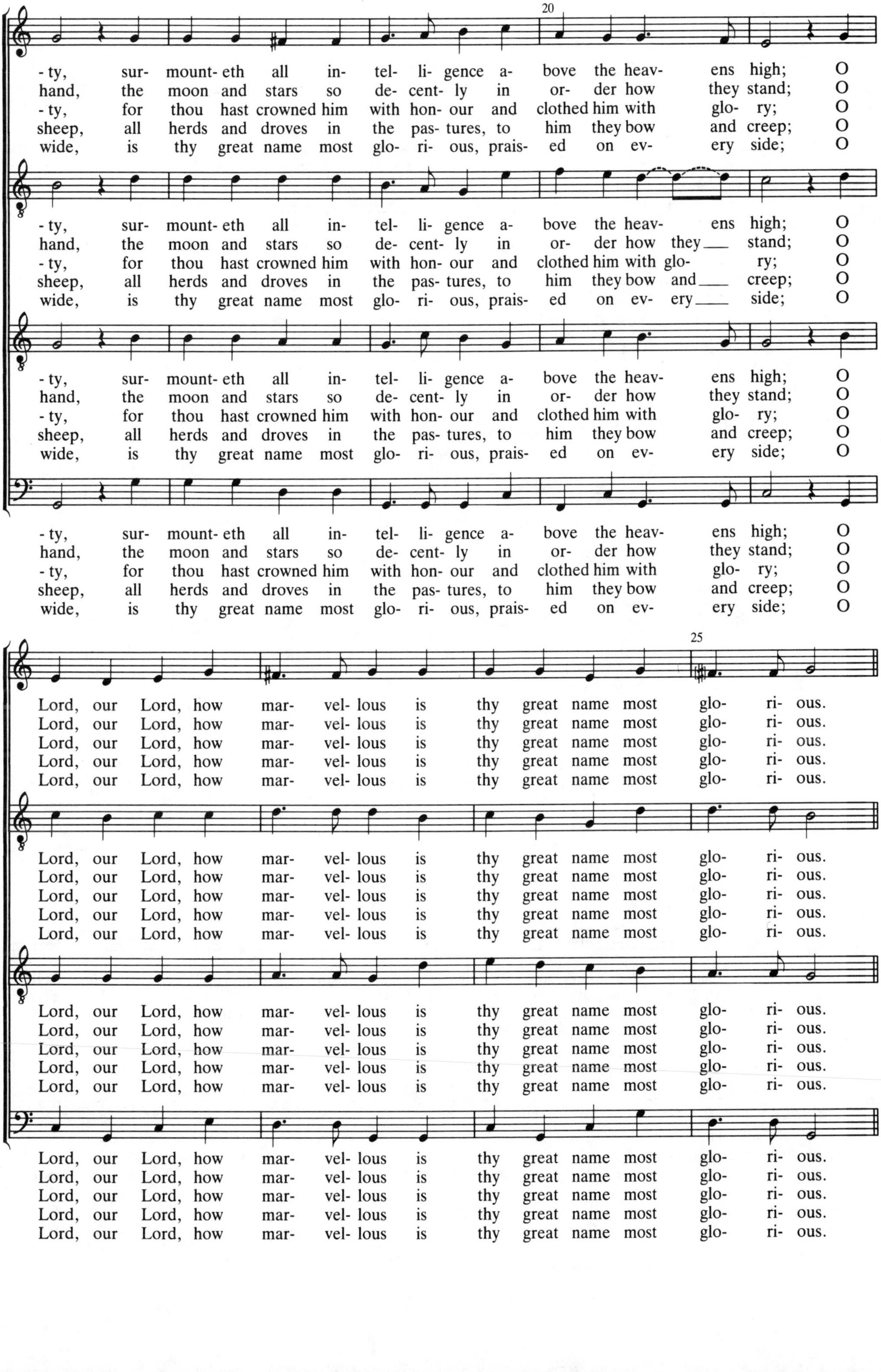
20
- ty, sur- mount- eth all in- tel- li- gence a- bove the heav- ens high; O
hand, the moon and stars so de- cent- ly in or- der how they stand; O
- ty, for thou hast crowned him with hon- our and clothed him with glo- ry; O
sheep, all herds and droves in the pas- tures, to him they bow and creep; O
wide, is thy great name most glo- ri- ous, prais- ed on ev- ery side; O
- ty, sur- mount- eth all in- tel- li- gence a- bove the heav- ens high; O
hand, the moon and stars so de- cent- ly in or- der how they___ stand; O
- ty, for thou hast crowned him with hon- our and clothed him with glo- ry; O
sheep, all herds and droves in the pas- tures, to him they bow and___ creep; O
wide, is thy great name most glo- ri- ous, prais- ed on ev- ery___ side; O
- ty, sur- mount- eth all in- tel- li- gence a- bove the heav- ens high; O
hand, the moon and stars so de- cent- ly in or- der how they stand; O
- ty, for thou hast crowned him with hon- our and clothed him with glo- ry; O
sheep, all herds and droves in the pas- tures, to him they bow and creep; O
wide, is thy great name most glo- ri- ous, prais- ed on ev- ery side; O
- ty, sur- mount- eth all in- tel- li- gence a- bove the heav- ens high; O
hand, the moon and stars so de- cent- ly in or- der how they stand; O
- ty, for thou hast crowned him with hon- our and clothed him with glo- ry; O
sheep, all herds and droves in the pas- tures, to him they bow and creep; O
wide, is thy great name most glo- ri- ous, prais- ed on ev- ery side; O
25
Lord, our Lord, how mar- vel- lous is thy great name most glo- ri- ous.
Lord, our Lord, how mar- vel- lous is thy great name most glo- ri- ous.
Lord, our Lord, how mar- vel- lous is thy great name most glo- ri- ous.
Lord, our Lord, how mar- vel- lous is thy great name most glo- ri- ous.
Lord, our Lord, how mar- vel- lous is thy great name most glo- ri- ous.
Lord, our Lord, how mar- vel- lous is thy great name most glo- ri- ous.
Lord, our Lord, how mar- vel- lous is thy great name most glo- ri- ous.
Lord, our Lord, how mar- vel- lous is thy great name most glo- ri- ous.
Lord, our Lord, how mar- vel- lous is thy great name most glo- ri- ous.
Lord, our Lord, how mar- vel- lous is thy great name most glo- ri- ous.
Lord, our Lord, how mar- vel- lous is thy great name most glo- ri- ous.
Lord, our Lord, how mar- vel- lous is thy great name most glo- ri- ous.
Lord, our Lord, how mar- vel- lous is thy great name most glo- ri- ous.
Lord, our Lord, how mar- vel- lous is thy great name most glo- ri- ous.
Lord, our Lord, how mar- vel- lous is thy great name most glo- ri- ous.
Lord, our Lord, how mar- vel- lous is thy great name most glo- ri- ous.
Lord, our Lord, how mar- vel- lous is thy great name most glo- ri- ous.
Lord, our Lord, how mar- vel- lous is thy great name most glo- ri- ous.
Lord, our Lord, how mar- vel- lous is thy great name most glo- ri- ous.
Lord, our Lord, how mar- vel- lous is thy great name most glo- ri- ous.

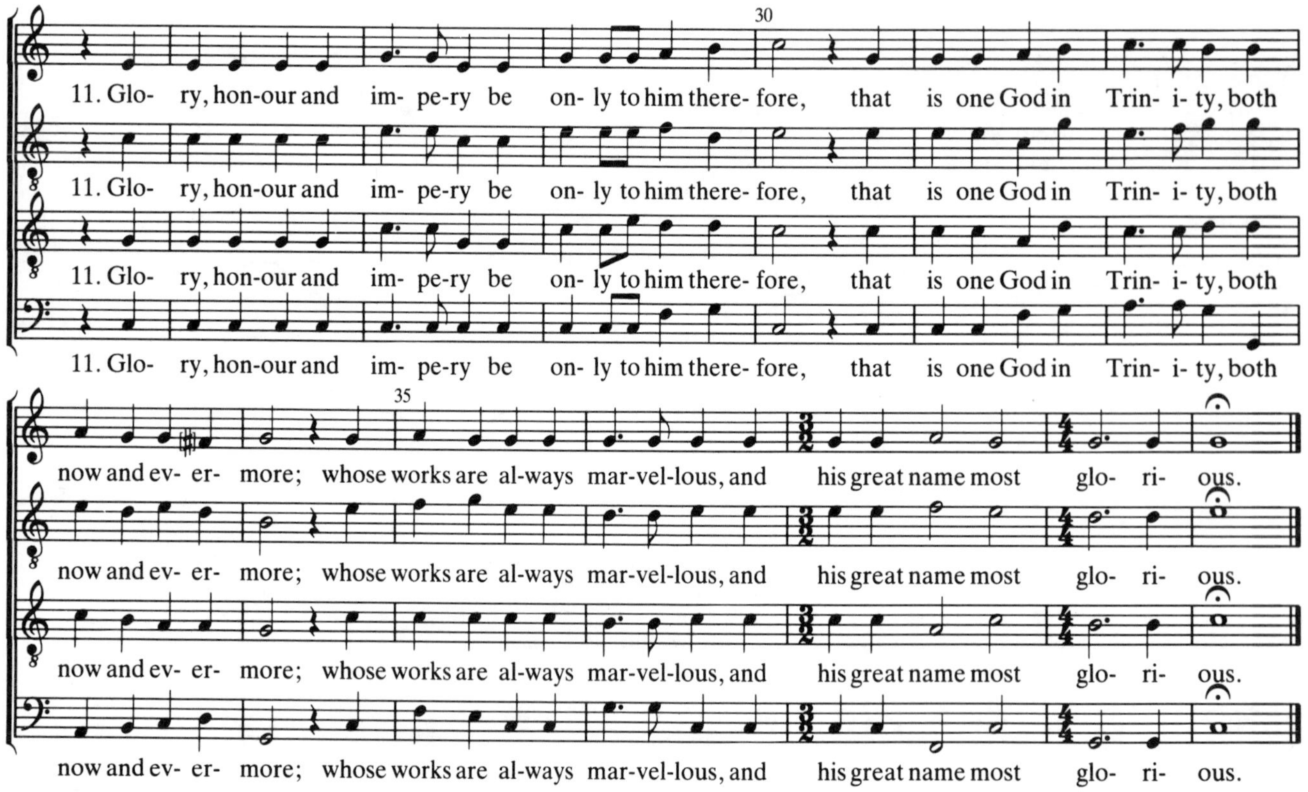

[18] Usquequo Domine

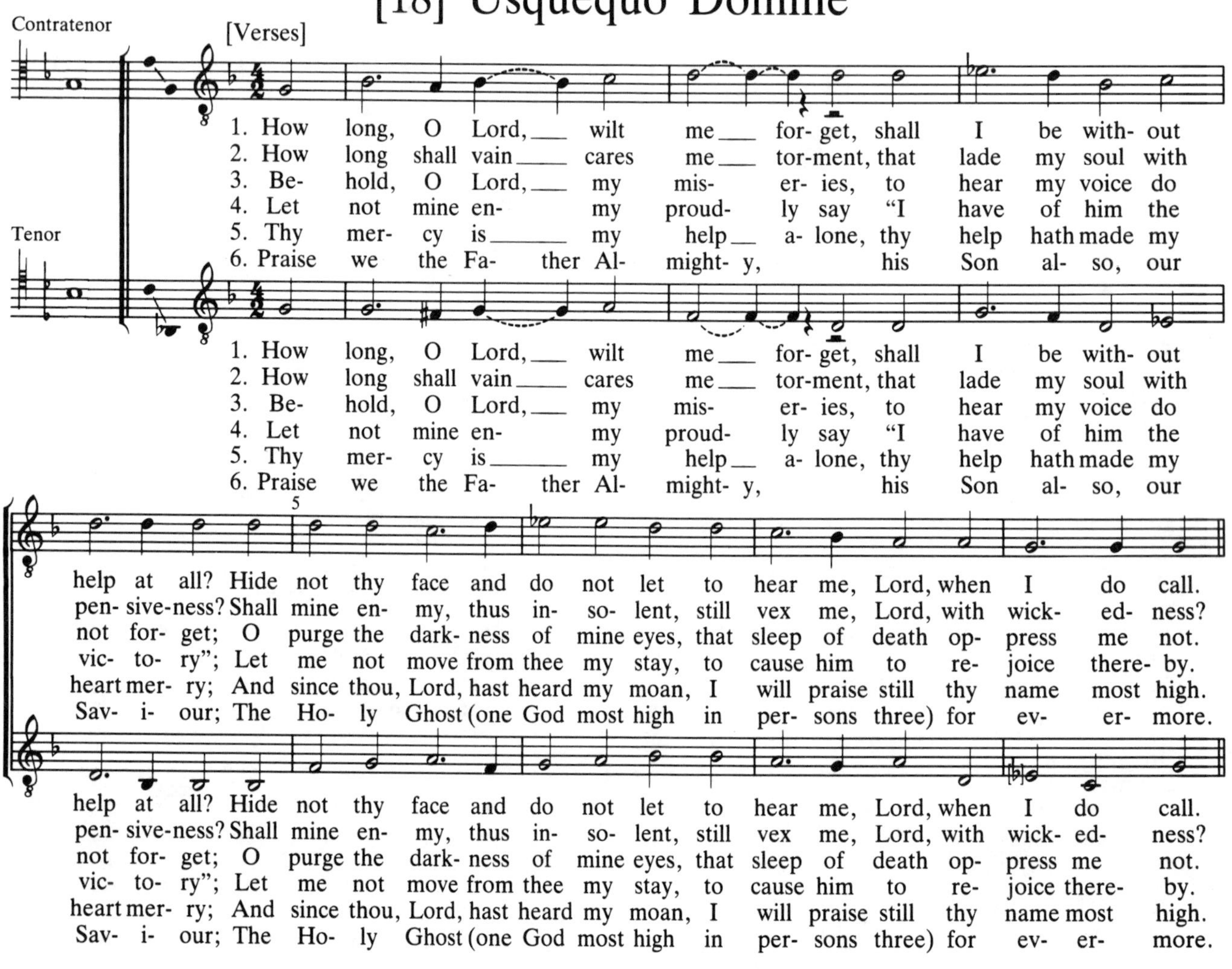

[Burden]
Triplex
Contratenor
Tenor
[Bassus]
10
How long, O Lord, wilt me for- get, shall I be with- out
How long, O Lord, wilt me for- get, shall I be with- out
How long, O Lord, wilt me for- get, shall I be with- out
How long, O Lord, wilt me for- get, shall I be with- out
15
help at all? Hide not thy face and do not let to hear me, Lord, when I do call.
help at all? Hide not thy face and do not let to hear me, Lord, when I do call.
help at all? Hide not thy face and do not let to hear me, Lord, when I do call.
help at all? Hide not thy face and do not let to hear me, Lord, when I do call.
[Alternative version of verse 6]
Triplex
Contratenor
[Bassus]
We praise the Fa- ther Al- might- y, his Son al- so our
We praise the Fa- ther Al- might- y, his Son al- so our
We praise the Fa- ther Al- might- y, his Son al- so our
20
Sav- i- our; the Ho- ly Ghost (one God most high in per-sons three) for ev- er- more.
Sav- i- our; the Ho- ly Ghost (one God most high in per- sons three) for ev- er-more.
Sav- i- our; the Ho- ly Ghost (one God most high in per-sons three) for ev- er- more.

[19] Celi enarrant

10
-ship doth tes- ti- fy, each day doth show thy prov- i- dence,
heav- ens from hour to hour, from east to west his course is set,
are in blind- ness laid, his ho- ly fear most clear and light,
I think no griev- ance, O keep me, Lord, that wit- ting- ly
-ship doth tes- ti- fy, each day doth show thy prov- i- dence,
heav- ens from hour to hour, from east to west his course is set,
are in blind- ness laid, his ho- ly fear most clear and light,
I think no griev- ance, O keep me, Lord, that wit- ting- ly
-ship doth tes- ti- fy, each day doth show thy prov- i- dence,
heav- ens from hour to hour, from east to west his course is set,
are in blind- ness laid, his ho- ly fear most clear and light,
I think no griev- ance, O keep me, Lord, that wit- ting- ly
-ship doth tes- ti- fy, each day doth show thy prov- i- dence,
heav- ens from hour to hour, from east to west his course is set,
are in blind- ness laid, his ho- ly fear most clear and light,
I think no griev- ance, O keep me, Lord, that wit- ting- ly
15
each night in course as they en- sue, thy power to us still they re- new.
whose power in things hath such de- gree, that from his heat none can be free.
con- tin- ueth still al- ways to en- dure, his laws are just, true, firm and sure.
I sin not and there- by do fall, in dan- ger of death e- ter- nal.
each night in course as they en- sue, thy power to us still they re- new.
whose power in things hath such de- gree, that from his heat none can be free.
con- tin- ueth still al- ways to en- dure, his laws are just, true, firm and sure.
I sin not and there- by do fall, in dan- ger of death e- ter- nal.
each night in course as they en- sue, thy power to us still they re- new.
whose power in things hath such de- gree, that from his heat none can be free.
con- tin- ueth still al- ways to en- dure, his laws are just, true, firm and sure.
I sin not and there- by do fall, in dan- ger of death e- ter- nal.
each night in course as they en- sue, thy power to us still they re- new.
whose power in things hath such de- gree, that from his heat none can be free.
con- tin- ueth still al- ways to en- dure, his laws are just, true, firm and sure.
I sin not and there- by do fall, in dan- ger of death e- ter- nal.

20
2. The heav- ens have no voice nor sound to ex- press by words their mak- er's
4. Yet though the sun and heav- ens high God's might- y power so much ex-
6. Thy laws ex- cel all gems and gold, how fine and pure so ev- er they
8. Both pure and clear then shall I be, and void from each griev- ous de-
2. The heav- ens have no voice nor sound to ex- press by words their mak- er's
4. Yet though the sun and heav- ens high God's might- y power so much ex-
6. Thy laws ex- cel all gems and gold, how fine and pure so ev- er they
8. Both pure and clear then shall I be, and void from each griev- ous de-
2. The heav- ens have no voice nor sound to ex- press by words their mak- er's
4. Yet though the sun and heav- ens high God's might- y power so much ex-
6. Thy laws ex- cel all gems and gold, how fine and pure so ev- er they
8. Both pure and clear then shall I be, and void from each griev- ous de-
2. The heav- ens have no voice nor sound to ex- press by words their mak- er's
4. Yet though the sun and heav- ens high God's might- y power so much ex-
6. Thy laws ex- cel all gems and gold, how fine and pure so ev- er they
8. Both pure and clear then shall I be, and void from each griev- ous de-
25
might, his works do yet his power ex- pound through all the
- press, the Lord's law much more mar- vel- lous- ly doth still re-
be, more sweet than hon- ey a thou- sand- fold, or hon- ey-
- sert, O let the words I speak to thee, and med- i-
might, his works do yet his power ex- pound through all the
- press, the Lord's law much more mar- vel- lous- ly doth still re-
be, more sweet than hon- ey a thou- sand- fold, or hon- ey-
- sert, O let the words I speak to thee, and med- i-
might, his works do yet his power ex- pound through all the
- press, the Lord's law much more mar- vel- lous- ly doth still re-
be, more sweet than hon- ey a thou- sand- fold, or hon- ey-
- sert, O let the words I speak to thee, and med- i-
might, his works do yet his power ex- pound through all the
- press, the Lord's law much more mar- vel- lous- ly doth still re-
be, more sweet than hon- ey a thou- sand- fold, or hon- ey-
- sert, O let the words I speak to thee, and med- i-

30
earth both day and night, a prince- ly throne there he hath found, where he hath
- vive our minds doubt- less, the Lord's law turns our souls tru- ly, his doc- trine
- comb be- yond de- gree, O Lord, by them thou hast me told that who- so
- ta- tion of my heart be pleas- ant to thy maj- es- ty, O Lord my
earth both day and night, a prince- ly throne there he hath found, where he hath
- vive our minds doubt- less, the Lord's law turns our souls tru- ly, his doc- trine
- comb be- yond de- gree, O Lord, by them thou hast me told that who- so
- ta- tion of my heart be pleas- ant to thy maj- es- ty, O Lord my
earth both day and night, a prince- ly throne there he hath found, where he hath
- vive our minds doubt- less, the Lord's law turns our souls tru- ly, his doc- trine
- comb be- yond de- gree, O Lord, by them thou hast me told that who- so
- ta- tion of my heart be pleas- ant to thy maj- es- ty, O Lord my
earth both day and night, a prince- ly throne there he hath found, where he hath
- vive our minds doubt- less, the Lord's law turns our souls tru- ly, his doc- trine
- comb be- yond de- gree, O Lord, by them thou hast me told that who- so
- ta- tion of my heart be pleas- ant to thy maj- es- ty, O Lord my
put the sun in place, most ___ pleas- ant- ly to run his race.
is al- ways con- stant, teach- ing wis- dom to the ig- no- rant.
keep them shall pur- chase a ___ great re- ward in thy pal- ace.
God, my rock, my stone, my re- deem- er and my hope a- lone.
put the sun in place, most ___ pleas- ant- ly to run his ___ race.
is al- ways con- stant, teach- ing wis- dom to the ig- no- rant.
keep them shall pur- chase a ___ great re- ward in thy pal- ace.
God, my rock, my stone, my re- deem- er and my hope a- lone.
put the sun in place, most ___ pleas- ant- ly to run his ___ race.
is al- ways con- stant, teach- ing wis- dom to the ig- no- rant.
keep them shall pur- chase a ___ great re- ward in thy pal- ace.
God, my rock, my stone, my re- deem- er and my hope a- lone.
put the sun in place, most ___ pleas- ant- ly to run his ___ race.
is al- ways con- stant, teach- ing wis- dom to the ig- no- rant.
keep them shall pur- chase a ___ great re- ward in thy pal- ace.
God, my rock, my stone, my re- deem- er and my hope a- lone.

[20] Domine quis

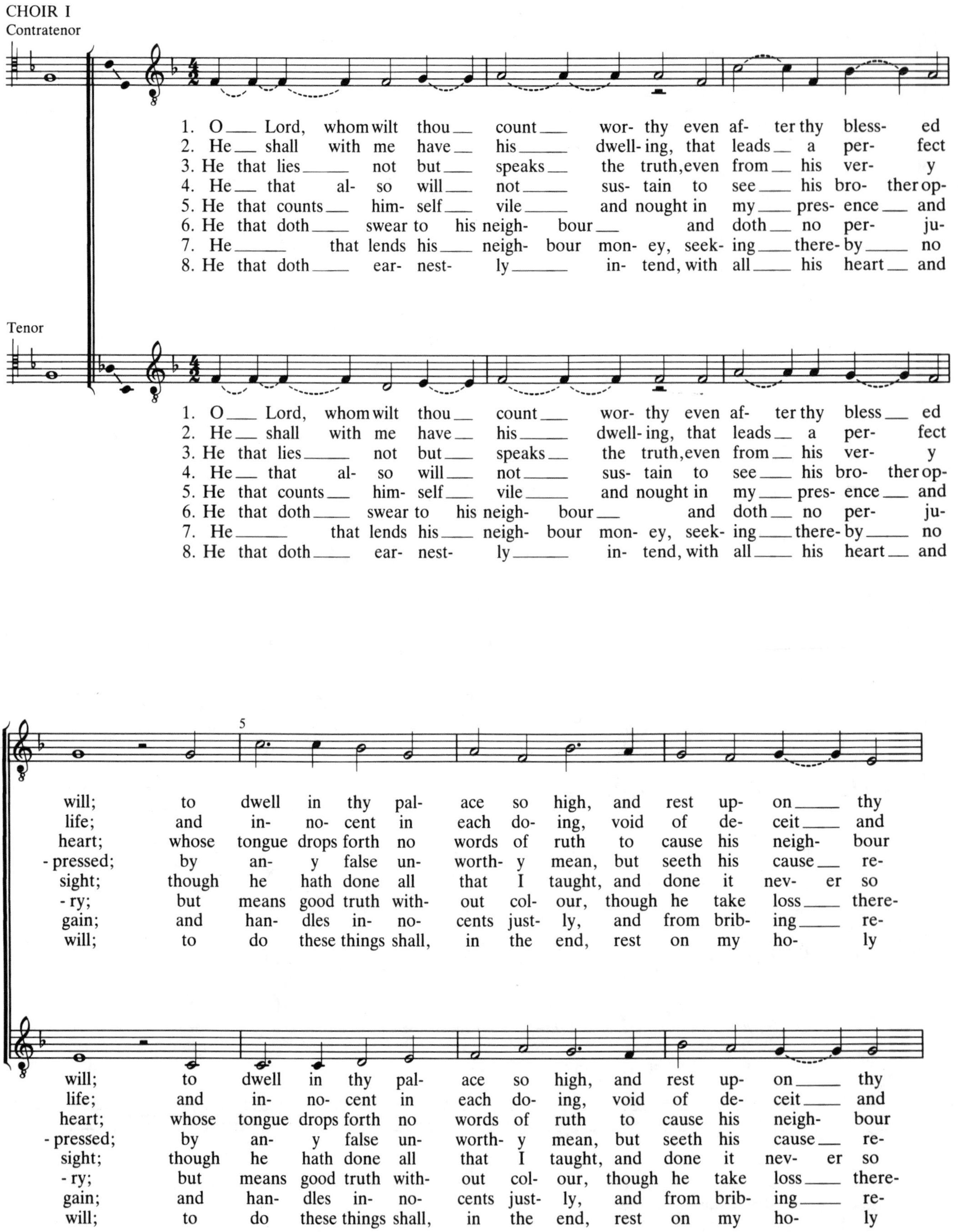
CHOIR I
Contratenor
1. O Lord, whom wilt thou count wor- thy even af- ter thy bless- ed
2. He shall with me have his dwell- ing, that leads a per- fect
3. He that lies not but speaks the truth, even from his ver- y
4. He that al- so will not sus- tain to see his bro- ther op-
5. He that counts him- self vile and nought in my pres- ence and
6. He that doth swear to his neigh- bour and doth no per- ju-
7. He that lends his neigh- bour mon- ey, seek- ing there- by no
8. He that doth ear- nest- ly in- tend, with all his heart and
Tenor
1. O Lord, whom wilt thou count wor- thy even af- ter thy bless ed
2. He shall with me have his dwell- ing, that leads a per- fect
3. He that lies not but speaks the truth, even from his ver- y
4. He that al- so will not sus- tain to see his bro- ther op-
5. He that counts him- self vile and nought in my pres- ence and
6. He that doth swear to his neigh- bour and doth no per- ju-
7. He that lends his neigh- bour mon- ey, seek- ing there- by no
8. He that doth ear- nest- ly in- tend, with all his heart and
5
will; to dwell in thy pal- ace so high, and rest up- on thy
life; and in- no- cent in each do- ing, void of de- ceit and
heart; whose tongue drops forth no words of ruth to cause his neigh- bour
- pressed; by an- y false un- worth- y mean, but seeth his cause re-
sight; though he hath done all that I taught, and done it nev- er so
- ry; but means good truth with- out col- our, though he take loss there-
gain; and han- dles in- no- cents just- ly, and from brib- ing re-
will; to do these things shall, in the end, rest on my ho- ly
will; to dwell in thy pal- ace so high, and rest up- on thy
life; and in- no- cent in each do- ing, void of de- ceit and
heart; whose tongue drops forth no words of ruth to cause his neigh- bour
- pressed; by an- y false un- worth- y mean, but seeth his cause re-
sight; though he hath done all that I taught, and done it nev- er so
- ry; but means good truth with- out col- our, though he take loss there-
gain; and han- dles in- no- cents just- ly, and from brib- ing re-
will; to do these things shall, in the end, rest on my ho- ly

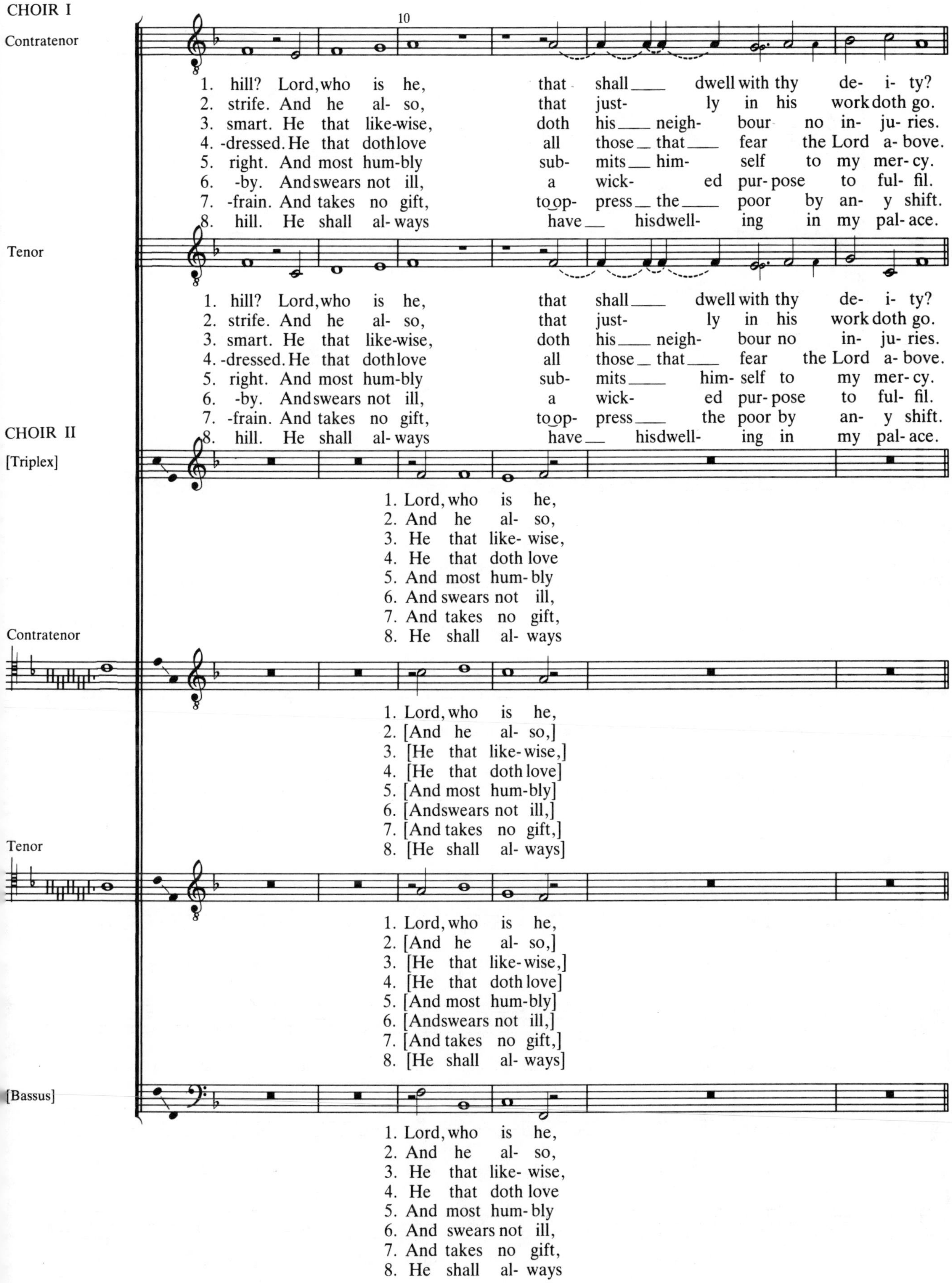
CHOIR I
Contratenor
10
1. hill? Lord, who is he, that shall dwell with thy de- i- ty?
2. strife. And he al- so, that just- ly in his work doth go.
3. smart. He that like-wise, doth his neigh- bour no in- ju- ries.
4. -dressed. He that doth love all those that fear the Lord a- bove.
5. right. And most hum-bly sub- mits him- self to my mer- cy.
6. -by. And swears not ill, a wick- ed pur- pose to ful- fil.
7. -frain. And takes no gift, to op- press the poor by an- y shift.
8. hill. He shall al- ways have his dwell- ing in my pal- ace.
Tenor
1. hill? Lord, who is he, that shall dwell with thy de- i- ty?
2. strife. And he al- so, that just- ly in his work doth go.
3. smart. He that like-wise, doth his neigh- bour no in- ju- ries.
4. -dressed. He that doth love all those that fear the Lord a- bove.
5. right. And most hum-bly sub- mits him- self to my mer- cy.
6. -by. And swears not ill, a wick- ed pur- pose to ful- fil.
7. -frain. And takes no gift, to op- press the poor by an- y shift.
8. hill. He shall al- ways have his dwell- ing in my pal- ace.
CHOIR II
[Triplex]
1. Lord, who is he,
2. And he al- so,
3. He that like- wise,
4. He that doth love
5. And most hum- bly
6. And swears not ill,
7. And takes no gift,
8. He shall al- ways
Contratenor
1. Lord, who is he,
2. [And he al- so,]
3. [He that like- wise,]
4. [He that doth love]
5. [And most hum-bly]
6. [And swears not ill,]
7. [And takes no gift,]
8. [He shall al- ways]
Tenor
1. Lord, who is he,
2. [And he al- so,]
3. [He that like- wise,]
4. [He that doth love]
5. [And most hum-bly]
6. [And swears not ill,]
7. [And takes no gift,]
8. [He shall al- ways]
[Bassus]
1. Lord, who is he,
2. And he al- so,
3. He that like- wise,
4. He that doth love
5. And most hum- bly
6. And swears not ill,
7. And takes no gift,
8. He shall al- ways

Triplex
Contratenor
Tenor
[Bassus]
[Burden]
CHOIR II
15
O Lord, whom wilt thou count wor- thy even af- ter thy bless- ed
20
will; to dwell in thy pal- ace so high, and rest up- on thy hill? Lord,
CHOIR I
25
who is he, Lord, who is he, that shall dwell with thy de- i- ty?

[21] [O Lord rebuke me not]

30
heal me, Lord, for my bones are bruis- ed, heal me, Lord, for my bones are
Lord, [heal me, Lord,] for my bones are bruis- ed, heal me, Lord, for my bones are
Lord, heal me, Lord, for my bones are bruis- ed, heal me, Lord, for my bones are
Lord, heal me, Lord, for my bones are bruis- ed, heal me, Lord, for my bones are
35
bruis- ed. And my soul is ver-y sore trou- bled, is ver- y sore trou-bled:
bruis- ed. And my soul is ver-y sore trou- bled, is ver- y sore trou-bled:
bruis- ed. And my soul is ver-y sore trou- bled, is ver- y sore trou-bled:
bruis- ed. And my soul is ver-y sore trou- bled, is ver- y sore trou-bled:
40
but how long, how long, Lord, how long, Lord? Turn thee, Lord, turn thee,
but how long, how long, Lord, how long, Lord? Turn thee, Lord, turn thee,
but how long, how long, Lord, how long, Lord? Turn thee, Lord, turn thee,
but how long, how long, Lord, how long, Lord? Turn thee, Lord, turn thee,
45
Lord, turn thee, Lord, and de- - liv- er my soul: save me for thy
Lord, turn thee, Lord, and de- liv- er my soul: save me for thy
Lord, turn thee, Lord, and de- liv- er my soul: save me for thy
Lord, turn thee, Lord, and de- liv- er my soul: save me for thy

50
55
mer- cy sake, save me for thy mer- cy sake, save me for thy mer- cy sake. For
mer- cy sake, save me for thy mer- cy sake, save me for thy mer- cy sake.
mer- cy sake, save me for thy mer- cy sake, save me for thy mer- cy sake. For
mer- cy sake, save me for thy mer- cy sake, save me for thy mer- cy sake.
60
there is none in death that hath mind of thee: and in hell who will
that hath mind of thee: and in hell who will
there is none in death that hath mind of thee: and in hell who will
that hath mind of thee: and in hell who will
65
knowl-edge thee, who will knowl- edge thee?
knowl-edge thee, who will knowl- edge thee? I have tra-vail-ed in my
knowl-edge thee, who will knowl- edge thee? I have tra-vail-ed in my
knowl-edge thee, who will knowl- edge thee?
70
I have la- bour-ed in my sor- rows;
wail-ing and mourn- ing, I have la- bour-ed in my sor- rows;
wail-ing and mourn- ing, I have la- bour-ed in my sor- rows; I shall
I have la- bour-ed in my sor- rows; I shall

75
I shall ev- e- ry night wash my bed with tears:
I shall ev- e- ry night wash my bed with tears: with
ev- e- ry night wash my bed with tears:
ev- e- ry night wash my bed with tears: with
with tears shall I wet the
tears shall I wet, with tears shall I wet the place where I lie, the
with tears shall I wet the place where I lie, the
tears shall I wet, with tears shall I wet the
80
place where I lie. Mine eye is trou- bled, mine eye is trou- bled with wood-ness:
place where I lie. Mine eye is trou- bled, mine eye is trou- bled with wood-ness:
place where I lie. Mine eye is trou- bled, mine eye is trou- bled with wood-ness:
place where I lie. Mine eye is trou- bled, mine eye is trou- bled with wood-ness:
85
I have wax- en old a-mong mine en- e- mies, I have wax- en
I have wax- en old a-mong mine en- e- mies, I have wax- en
I have wax- en
I have wax- en old a- mong mine en- e- mies, I have wax- en

90
old a- mong mine en- e- mies, a- mong mine en- e- mies.
old a- mong mine en- e- mies, a- mong mine en- e- mies.
old a- mong mine en- e- mies, a- mong mine en- e- mies.
old a- mong mine en- e- mies, a- mong mine en- e- mies.
95
A- void from me, all you that work wick- ed-ness: for the Lord hath heard the
A- void from me, all you that work wick- ed-ness: for the Lord hath heard the
A- void from me, all you that work wick- ed-ness: for the Lord hath heard the
A- void from me, all you that work wick- ed-ness: for the Lord hath heard the
100
105
noise of my weep-ing. A- void from me, all you that work wick- ed-ness: for the
noise of my weep-ing. A- void from me, all you that work wick- ed-ness: for the
noise of my weep-ing. A- void from me, all you that work wick- ed-ness: for the
noise of my weep-ing. A- void from me, all you that work wick- ed-ness: for the
Lord hath heard the noise of my weep- ing, for the Lord hath heard the
Lord hath heard the noise of my weep- ing, for the Lord hath heard the
Lord hath heard the noise of my weep- ing, for the Lord hath heard the
Lord hath heard the noise of my weep- ing, for the Lord hath heard the

110
noise of my__ weep- ing. The Lord hath heard my
noise of my__ weep- ing. The Lord hath heard my
noise__ of my weep- ing. The Lord hath heard my
noise of my weep- ing. The Lord hath heard my
115
pray- er: the Lord hath heard my pe- ti- ti- on, my pe-
pray- er: the Lord hath heard my pe- ti- ti- on, my pe-
pray- er: the Lord hath heard my pe- ti- ti- on, my pe-
pray- er: the Lord hath heard my pe- ti- ti- on, my pe-
120
-ti- ti- on. Let all mine en- e-mies be a- sham-ed and con- found- ed,
-ti- ti- on. Let all mine en- e-mies be a- sham-ed and con- found- ed,
-ti- ti- on. Let all mine en- e-mies be a- sham-ed and con- found- ed,
-ti- ti- on. Let all mine en- e-mies be a- sham-ed and con- found- ed,
125
130
let all mine en- e-mies be a- sham- ed and con- found-ed ver- y quick-ly,
let all mine en- e-mies be a- sham- ed and con- found-ed ver- y quick-ly,
let all mine en- e-mies be a- sham- ed and con- found-ed ver- y quick-ly,
let all mine en- e-mies be a- sham- ed and con- found-ed ver- y quick-ly,

135
and con- found- ed ver- y quick- ly. Glo- ry be to the Fa-
and con- found- ed ver- y quick- ly. Glo- ry be to the Fa-
and con- found- ed ver- y quick- ly. Glo- ry be to the Fa-
and con- found- ed ver- y quick- ly. Glo- ry be to the Fa-
140
145
- ther and to the Son: and to the Ho- ly Ghost; As it was
- ther and to the Son: and to the Ho- ly Ghost; As it was
- ther and to the Son: and to the Ho- ly Ghost; As it was
- ther and to the Son: and to the Ho- ly Ghost; As it was
150
in the be- gin-ning, as it is now, as it is now and ev- er shall
in the be- gin-ning, as it is now, as it is, as it is now, as it is now and ev- er shall
in the be- gin-ning, as it is, as it is now, as it is now and ev- er shall
in the be- gin-ning, as it is now, as it is now and ev- er shall
155
160
be, and ev- - er shall be, and ev- er shall be: A- - men; and ev- er shall be: A- men.
be, and ev- - er shall be, and ev- er shall be: A- - men; and ev- er shall be: A- men.
be, and ev- - er shall be, and ev- er shall be: A- - men; and ev- er shall be: A- men.
be, and ev- er shall be: A- - men; and ev- er shall be: A- men.

[22] [O Lord Christ Jesu]

CHOIR II
25
CHOIR I
sin- ners do most hum-bly, we sin- ners do most hum-bly, be- seech thy high maj- es-
sin- ners do most hum-bly, we sin- ners do most hum-bly, be- seech thy high maj- es-
sin- ners do most hum-bly, we sin- ners do most hum-bly, be- seech thy high maj- es-
sin- ners do most hum-bly, we sin- ners do most hum-bly, be- seech thy high maj- es-
30
CHOIR II
CHOIR I
35
- ty, be- seech thy high maj- es- - ty to grant thy no- ble ser- vant our
- ty, be- seech thy high maj- es- - ty to grant thy no- ble ser-vant our
- ty, be- seech thy high maj- es- ty to grant thy no- ble ser- vant our
- ty, be- seech thy high maj- es- ty to grant thy no- ble ser- vant our
CHOIR II
40
sov-ereign lord King Ed- ward, King Ed- ward, to grant thy no- ble ser- vant our
sov-ereign lord King Ed- ward, King Ed- ward, to grant thy no- ble ser- vant our
sov-ereign lord King Ed- ward, King Ed- ward, to grant thy no- ble ser- vant our
sov-ereign lord King Ed- ward, King Ed- ward, to grant thy no- ble ser- vant our
CHOIR I, II
45
sov- ereign lord King Ed- ward, King Ed- ward, our sov- ereign lord King Ed- ward;
sov- ereign lord King Ed- ward, King Ed- ward, our sov- ereign lord King Ed- ward;
sov- ereign lord King Ed- ward, King Ed- ward, our sov- ereign lord King Ed- ward;
sov- ereign lord King Ed- ward, King Ed- ward, our sov- ereign lord King Ed- ward;

CHOIR I
CHOIR II
50
CHOIR I
that he may have tho-rough thee, that he may have tho-rough thee o- ver
that he may have tho-rough thee, that he may have tho-rough thee o- ver
that he may have tho-rough thee, that he may have tho-rough thee o- ver
that he may have tho-rough thee, that he may have tho-rough thee o- ver
CHOIR II
55
CHOIR I
60
CHOIR II
all his en- e- mies, o- ver all his en- e- mies most roy- al vic- to- ry, most roy- al
all his en- e- mies, o- ver all his en- e- mies most roy- al vic- to- ry, most roy- al
all his en- e- mies, o- ver all his en- e- mies most roy- al vic- to- ry, most roy- al
all his en- e- mies, o- ver all his en- e- mies most roy- al vic- to- ry, most roy- al
CHOIR I, II
65
CHOIR I
CHOIR II
CHOIR I, II
vic- to- ry, most roy- al vic- to-ry. Yet fur-ther- more, yet fur- ther- more, to
vic- to- ry, most roy- al vic- - to-ry. Yet fur-ther- more, yet fur- ther- more, to
vic- to- ry, most roy- al vic- to-ry. Yet fur-ther- more, yet fur- ther- more, to
vic- to- ry, most roy- al vic- to-ry. Yet fur-ther- more, yet fur- ther- more, to
70
75
thee, O Lord, we do both cry and call, we do both cry and
thee, O Lord, we do both cry and call, we do both cry and
thee, O Lord, we do both cry and call, we do both cry and
thee, O Lord, we do both cry and call, we do both cry and

80
call, that thou wilt as- sist him, that thou wilt as- sist him in
call, that thou wilt as- sist him, that thou wilt as- sist him in
call, that thou wilt as- sist him, that thou wilt as- sist him in
call, that thou wilt as- sist him, that thou wilt as- sist him in
85
90
his af- - fairs all, in his af- - fairs all, in his af-
his af- fairs all, in his af- fairs all, in his af-
his af- fairs all, in his af- fairs all, in his af-
his af- fairs all, in his af- fairs all, in his af-
CHOIR I
- fairs all. O bless- ed Je- su, most might- i- est King im-
- fairs all. O bless- ed Je- su, most might- i- est King im-
- fairs all. O bless- ed Je- su, most might-iest King im-
- fairs all. O bless- ed Je- su, most might- i- est King im-
CHOIR II
CHOIR I, II
95
100
- mor- tal, O bless-ed Je- su, most might- i- est King im- mor- tal; stretch
- mor- tal, O bless-ed Je- su, most might- i- est King im- mor- tal; stretch
- mor- tal, O bless-ed Je- su, most might- i- est King im- mor- tal; stretch
- mor- tal, O bless-ed Je- su, most might- i- est King im- mor- tal; stretch

105
forth thy ho- ly hand through thy power po- ten- ti- al, in con-
forth thy ho- ly hand through thy power po- ten- ti- al, in con-
forth thy ho- ly hand through thy power po- ten- ti- al, in con-
forth thy ho- ly hand through thy power po- ten- ti- al, in con-
110
-found- ing of his en- e-mies for ev- er a me- mo- ri- al, in con- found- ing of his
-found- ing of his en- e-mies for ev- er a me- mo- ri- al, in con- found- ing of his
-found- ing of his en- e-mies for ev- er a me- mo- ri- al, in con- found- ing of his
-found- ing of his en- e-mies for ev- er a me- mo- ri- al, in con- found- ing of his
en- e- mies for ev- er a me- mo- ri- al, for ev- er a me- mo- ri-
en- e- mies for ev- er a me- mo- ri- al, for ev- er a me- mo- ri-
en- e- mies for ev- er a me- mo- ri- al, for ev- er a me- mo- ri-
en- e- mies for ev- er a me- mo- ri- al, for ev- er a me- mo- ri-
115
CHOIR II
CHOIR I
120
-al. That we may sing with joy con- tin- u- al, that we may
-al. That we may sing with joy con- tin- u- al, that we may
-al. That we may sing with joy con- tin- u- al, that we may
-al. That we may sing with joy con- tin- u- al, that we may

CHOIR I, II
125
sing with joy con- tin- u- al, that we may sing with joy con- tin- u- al.
sing with joy con- tin- u- al, that we may sing with joy con- tin- u- al.
sing with joy con- tin- u- al, that we may sing with joy con- tin- u- al.
sing with joy con- tin- u- al, that we may sing with joy con- tin- u- al.
CHOIR I
130
CHOIR II
Bless- ed be the Lord ce- les- ti- al, bless- ed be the
Bless- ed be the Lord ce- les- ti- al, bless- ed be the
Bless- ed be the Lord ce- les- ti- al, bless- ed be the
Bless- ed be the Lord ce- les- ti- al, bless- ed be the
135
CHOIR I, II
140
Lord ce- les- ti- al, bless- ed be the Lord ce- les- ti-
Lord ce- les- ti- al, bless- ed be the Lord ce- les- ti-
Lord ce- les- ti- al, bless- ed be the Lord ce- les- ti-
Lord ce- les- ti- al, bless- ed be the Lord ce- les- ti-
145
-al, ce- les- ti- al: Al- ways so be it.
-al, ce- les- ti- al: Al- ways so be it.
-al, ce- les- ti- al: Al- ways so be it, so be it.
-al, ce- les- ti- al: Al- ways so be it.

[23] [Praised be God]

CHOIR II
15
sav- i- our, our sav- i- our, our sav- i- our. We are sin- ners,
sav- i- our, our sav- i- our, our sav- i- our. We are sin- ners,
sav- i- our, our sav- i- our, our sav- i- our. We are sin- ners,
sav- i- our, our sav- i- our, our sav- i- our. We are sin- ners,
we are sin- ners; un- righ- teous, fool-ish and flesh- ly, un- righ- teous,
we are sin- ners; un- righ- teous, fool-ish and flesh- ly, un- righ- teous,
we are sin- ners; un- righ- teous, fool-ish and flesh- ly, un- righ- teous,
we are sin- ners; un- righ- teous, fool-ish and flesh- ly, un- righ- teous,
20
CHOIR I
fool-ish and flesh- ly. Christ is our mer- cy stool, Christ is our mer- cy stool; our
fool-ish and flesh- ly. Christ is our mer- cy stool, Christ is our_ mer- cy stool; our
fool-ish and flesh- ly. Christ is our mer- cy stool, Christ is our_ mer- cy stool; our
fool-ish and flesh- ly. Christ is our mer- cy stool, Christ is our mer- cy stool; our
25
righ- teous-ness and our wis- dom ver- i- ly, our righ- teous-ness, our righ- teous-ness, our
righ- teous-ness and our wis- dom ver- i- ly, our righ- teous-ness, our righ- teous-ness, our
righ- teous-ness and our wis- dom_ ver- i- ly, our righ- teous-ness, our righ- teous-ness, our
righ- teous-ness and our wis- dom ver- i- ly, our righ- teous-ness, our righ- teous-ness, our

CHOIR II
30
righ- teous-ness and our wis- dom ver- i- ly, ver- i- ly. We are un- clean, hold- en un- der the
righ- teous-ness and our wis- dom ver- i- ly, ver- i- ly. We are un- clean, hold- en un- der the
righ- teous-ness and our wis- dom ver- i- ly, ver- i- ly. We are un- clean, hold- en un- der the
righ- teous-ness and our wis- dom ver- i- ly, ver- i- ly. We are un- clean, hold- en un- der the
35
dan- ger of death and sin, hold- en un- der the dan- ger of death and sin's ex- ac- ti- on.
dan- ger of death and sin, hold- en un- der the dan- ger of death and sin's ex- ac- ti- on.
dan- ger of death and sin, hold- en un- der the dan- ger of death and sin's ex- ac- ti- on.
dan- ger of death and sin, hold- en un- der the dan- ger of death and sin's ex- ac- ti- on.
CHOIR I
CHOIR II
40
CHOIR I, II
CHOIR I
Christ is our ho- li-ness, Christ is our ho- li-ness, Christ is our ho- li-ness; our
Christ is our ho- li-ness, Christ is our ho- li-ness, Christ is our ho- li-ness; our
Christ is our ho- li-ness, Christ is our ho- li-ness, Christ is our ho- li-ness; our
Christ is our ho- li-ness, Christ is our ho- li-ness, Christ is our ho- li-ness; our
CHOIR II
45
CHOIR I, II
life, our sat- is- fac- ti- on, our life, our sat- is- fac- ti- on, our life, our sat- is-
life, our sat- is- fac- ti- on, our life, our sat- is- fac- ti- on, our life, our sat- is-
life, our sat- is- fac- ti- on, our life, our sat- is- fac- ti- on, our life, our sat- is-
life, our sat- is- fac- ti- on, our life, our sat- is- fac- ti- on, our life, our sat- is-

CHOIR I
CHOIR II
CHOIR I, II
-fac- ti- on and re- demp- ti- on, and re- demp- ti- on, and re- demp- ti-
-fac- ti- on and re- demp- ti- on, and re- demp- ti- on, and re- demp- ti-
-fac- ti- on and re- demp- ti- on, and re- demp- ti- on, and re- demp- ti-
-fac- ti- on and re- demp- ti- on, and re- demp- ti- on, and re- demp- ti-
-on. Glo- ry be to thee, O Lord, glo- ry be to thee, O Lord; born of the
-on. Glo- ry be to thee, O Lord, glo- ry be to thee, O Lord; born of the
-on. Glo- ry be to thee, O Lord, glo- ry be to thee, O Lord; born of the
-on. Glo- ry be to thee, O Lord, glo- ry be to thee, O Lord; born of the
Vir-gin Ma- ry; glo- ry to the Fa- ther and to the Ho- ly Ghost; for ev- er and
Vir-gin Ma- ry; glo- ry to the Fa- ther and to the Ho- ly Ghost; for ev- er and
Vir-gin Ma- ry; glo- ry to the Fa- ther and to the Ho- ly Ghost; for ev- er and
Vir-gin Ma- ry; glo- ry to the Fa- ther and to the Ho- ly Ghost; for ev- er and
ev- er e- ter- nal-ly, for ev- er and ev- er e- ter- nal-ly. So be it.
ev- er e- ter- nal-ly, for ev- er and ev- er e- ter- nal-ly. So be it.
ev- er e- ter- nal-ly, for ev- er and ev- er e- ter- nal-ly. So be it.
ev- er e- ter- nal-ly, for ev- er and ev- er e- ter- nal-ly. So be it.

[24] [Benedicite]

15
- bove heaven, praise the Lord: all the Powers of the Lord, praise ye the Lord.
- bove heaven, praise the Lord: all the Powers of the Lord, praise ye the Lord.
- bove heaven, praise the Lord: all the Powers of the Lord, praise ye the Lord.
- bove heaven, praise the Lord: all the Powers of the Lord, praise ye the Lord.
CHOIR II
20
The Sun and Moon, praise ye the Lord: Stars of the Fir-ma-ment, praise ye the Lord.
The Sun and Moon, praise ye the Lord: Stars of the Fir-ma-ment, praise ye the Lord.
The Sun and Moon, praise ye the Lord: Stars of the Fir-ma-ment, praise ye the Lord.
The Sun and Moon, praise ye the Lord: Stars of the Fir-ma-ment, praise ye the Lord.
CHOIR I
25
The Rain and the Dew, praise ye the Lord: all ye Winds of God, praise ye the Lord.
The Rain and the Dew, praise ye the Lord: all ye Winds of God, praise ye the Lord.
The Rain and the Dew, praise ye the Lord: all ye Winds of God, praise ye the Lord.
The Rain and the Dew, praise ye the Lord: all ye Winds of God, praise ye the Lord.
CHOIR II
30
Fire and Heat, praise ye the Lord: Win-ter and Sum-mer, praise ye the Lord.
CHOIR I
Dews and Hoar-frosts,
Fire and Heat, praise ye the Lord: Win-ter and Sum- mer, praise ye the Lord. Dews and Hoar-frosts,
Fire and Heat, praise ye the Lord: Win-ter and Sum- mer, praise ye the Lord. Dews and Hoar-frosts,
Fire and Heat, praise ye the Lord: Win-ter and Sum- mer, praise ye the Lord. Dews and Hoar-frosts,

35
CHOIR II
40
praise ye the Lord: Frost and Cold, praise ye the Lord. Ice and Snow, praise ye the
praise ye the Lord: Frost and Cold, praise ye the Lord. Ice and Snow, praise ye the
praise ye the Lord: Frost and Cold, praise ye the Lord. Ice and Snow, praise ye the
praise ye the Lord: Frost and Cold, praise ye the Lord. Ice and Snow, praise ye the
CHOIR I
45
Lord: Nights and Days, praise ye the Lord. Light and Dark-ness, praise ye the Lord: Light-nings and Clouds,
Lord: Nights and Days, praise ye the Lord. Light and Dark-ness, praise ye the Lord: Light-nings and Clouds,
Lord: Nights and Days, praise _ ye the Lord. Light and Dark-ness, praise ye the Lord: Light-nings and Clouds,
Lord: Nights and Days, praise ye the Lord. Light and Dark-ness, praise ye the Lord: Light-nings and Clouds,
CHOIR II
50
praise ye the Lord. The Earth praise the Lord: laud and ex- alt him for ev- er.
praise ye the Lord. The Earth praise the Lord: laud and ex- alt him for ev- er.
praise ye the Lord. The Earth praise the Lord: laud and ex- alt him for _ ev- er.
praise ye the Lord. The Earth praise the Lord: laud and ex- alt him for ev- er.
CHOIR I
55
Moun-tains and Hills, praise ye the Lord: all that spring up-on the Earth, praise ye the Lord.
Moun-tains and Hills, praise ye the Lord: all that spring up-on the Earth, praise ye the Lord.
Moun-tains and Hills, praise ye the Lord: all that spring up-on the Earth, praise ye the Lord.
Moun-tains and Hills, praise ye the Lord: all that spring up-on the Earth, praise ye the Lord.

CHOIR II
60
Ye Wells and Springs, praise the Lord: Seas and Floods, praise ye the Lord.
Ye Wells and Springs, praise the Lord: Seas and Floods, praise ye the Lord.
Ye Wells and Springs, praise the Lord: Seas and Floods, praise ye the Lord.
Ye Wells and Springs, praise the Lord: Seas and Floods, praise ye the Lord.
CHOIR I
65
70
Great Fish-es and all that move in the Wa-ters, praise ye the Lord: all Birds of the Air,
Great Fish-es and all that move in the Wa-ters, praise ye the Lord: all Birds of the Air,
Great Fish-es and all that move in the Wa-ters, praise ye the Lord: all Birds of the Air,
Great Fish-es and all that move in the Wa-ters, praise ye the Lord: all Birds of the Air,
CHOIR II
75
praise ye the Lord. All Beasts and Cat-tle, praise ye the Lord: ye Chil-dren of
praise ye the Lord. All Beasts and Cat-tle, praise ye the Lord: ye Chil-dren of
praise ye the Lord. All Beasts and Cat-tle, praise ye the Lord: ye Chil-dren of
praise ye the Lord. All Beasts and Cat-tle, praise ye the Lord: ye Chil-dren of
80
CHOIR I
Men, praise the Lord. Let Is-ra-el praise the Lord: laud him and ex-
Men, praise the Lord. Let Is-ra-el praise the Lord: laud him and ex-
Men, praise the Lord. Let Is-ra-el praise the Lord: laud him and ex-
Men, praise the Lord. Let Is-ra-el praise the Lord: laud him and ex-

85
CHOIR II
90
- alt him for ev- er-more. Ye Priests of the Lord, praise ye the _ Lord: ye
- alt him for ev- er-more. Ye Priests of the Lord, praise ye the _ Lord: ye
- alt him for _ ev- er-more. Ye Priests of the Lord, praise ye the Lord: ye
- alt him for ev- er-more. Ye Priests of the Lord, praise ye the Lord: ye
CHOIR I
95
Ser-vants of the Lord, praise ______ the Lord. Ye Spir-its and Souls of Righ-teous Men,
Ser-vants of the Lord, praise the Lord. Ye Spir-its and Souls of Righ-teous Men,
Ser-vants of the Lord, praise the Lord. Ye Spir-its and Souls of Righ-teous Men,
Ser-vants of the Lord, praise the Lord. Ye Spir-its and Souls of Righ-teous Men,
100
praise the Lord: ye Ho-ly and Meek in Heart, Meek in Heart, praise ______ the Lord.
praise the Lord: ye Ho-ly and Meek in Heart, Meek in Heart, praise the Lord.
praise _ the Lord: ye Ho-ly and Meek in Heart, Meek in Heart, praise the Lord.
praise _ the Lord: ye Ho-ly and Meek in Heart, Meek in Heart, praise the Lord.
CHOIR II
105
An-a- ni-as, Az-a- ri-as, Mi-sa-el, praise ye the Lord: laud and ex- alt him for ev- er-more.
An-a- ni-as, Az-a- ri-as, Mi-sa-el, praise ye the Lord: laud and ex- alt him for ev- er-more.
An-a- ni-as, Az-a- ri-as, Mi-sa-el, praise ye the Lord: laud and ex- alt him for _ ev- er-more.
An-a- ni-as, Az-a- ri-as, Mi-sa-el, praise ye the Lord: laud and ex- alt him for ev- er-more.

CHOIR I
110
115
Bless we the Fa- ther, the Son, and the Ho- ly Ghost: praise we him and ex- alt him for
Bless we the Fa- ther, the Son, and the Ho- ly Ghost: praise we him and ex- alt him for
Bless we the Fa- ther, the Son, and the Ho- ly Ghost: praise we him and ex- alt him for ev-
Bless we the Fa- ther, the Son, and the Ho- ly Ghost: praise we him and ex- alt him for
CHOIR I, II
120
ev- er- more. Bless-ed art thou, Lord, in the Fir-ma-ment of Heaven: thou art praise-
ev- er- more. Bless-ed art thou, Lord, in the Fir-ma-ment of Heaven: thou art praise-
- er- more. Bles-sed art thou, Lord, in the Fir-ma-ment of Heaven: thou art praise-
ev- er- more. Bless-ed art thou, Lord, in the Fir-ma-ment of Heaven: thou art praise-
125
130
- wor- thy, glo- ri- ous and ex- al- ted, world with-out end. A- - men.
- wor- thy, glo- ri- ous and ex- al- ted, world with-out end. A- - men.
- wor- thy, glo- ri- ous and ex- al- ted, world with-out end. A- - men.
- wor- thy, glo- ri- ous and ex- al- ted, world with-out end. A- - men.

[25] [1552 Kyrie]

[26] [Nunc dimittis]

25
thou hast pre- par- ed: be- fore the
thou hast pre- - par- ed: be- fore the face of
thou hast pre- par- ed: be- fore the face of all peo- - ple,
thou hast pre- par- ed: be- fore the face of all peo- ple,
30
face of all peo- ple, of all peo- ple; To be a light to light- en the
all peo- ple, of all peo- ple; To be a light to light- en the
be- fore the face of all peo- ple; To be a light to light- en the
be- fore the face of all peo- ple; To be a light to light- en the
Gen- tiles, to be a light to light- en the Gen- tiles:
Gen-tiles, to light- en the Gen- tiles: and to be the
Gen- tiles: and to be the glo- ry of thy peo- ple Is- ra- el, of thy peo-
Gen- tiles: and to be the glo- ry of thy peo- ple
35
and to be the glo- ry of thy peo-ple, and to be the
glo- ry of thy peo-ple Is- ra- el, and to be the glo- ry of thy peo-ple Is- ra-
- ple Is- ra-el, and to be the glo- ry of thy peo- ple, the glo- ry
Is- ra-el, and to be the glo- ry of thy peo-ple Is- ra-el,

40
glo- ry of thy peo- ple Is- ra- el. Glo- ry be to the Fa- ther, and to the
-el, thy peo- ple Is- ra- el. Glo- ry be to the Fa- ther, and to the
of thy peo- ple Is- - ra- el. Glo- ry be to the Fa- ther, and to the
thy peo- ple Is- ra- el. Glo- ry be to the Fa- ther, and to the
45
Son: and to the Ho- ly Ghost; As it was in the be- gin- ning, is now,
Son: and to the Ho- - ly Ghost; As it was in the be- gin- ning, is now,
Son: and to the Ho- - ly Ghost; As it was in the be-gin-ning, is now, and
Son: and to the Ho- ly Ghost; As it was in the be- gin- ning, is now, and
50
and ev- er shall be, and ev- er shall be, and
and ev- er shall be, and ev- er shall be, and
ev- er shall be: world with- out end, and ev- er shall be: world with- out end,
ev- er shall be: and ev- er shall be: world with- out end,
55
ev- er shall be: world with- - out end. A- - men.
ev- er shall be: world with- out end. A- - men.
and ev- er shall be: world with-out end. A- - - men.
and ev- er shall be: world with- out end. A- - men.

[27] [Benedictus]

[Thomas] Tallis

20
As he spake by the mouth of his holy pro- phets: ___
As he spake by the mouth of his ho- ly pro-phets: which
As he spake by the mouth of his ho- ly pro- - phets: which
spake by the mouth of his ho- ly pro- phets, of his ho- ly pro- phets:
_ which hath been since the world be- gan, the world be-
hath been since the world be- gan, which hath been since the
hath been since the world be- gan, which hath been since the world be- gan, be-
which hath been since the world be- gan, which hath been since the world be-
25
- gan; That we should be sav- ed from our en- e-
world be- gan; That we should be sav-ed from our en- e-mies; and from the
- gan; That we should be sav- ed from our en- e-
- gan; That we should be sav- ed from our en- e- mies; ___ and
30
- mies; and from the hands of all that hate ___ us; To per- form the mer-
hands of all that hate _ us; To per- form the mer- cy prom-is- ed to our
- mies; and from the hands of all that hate _ us; To per-
from the hands of all that hate ___ us; To per- form the mer- cy prom-is-ed to our

35
- cy prom- is- ed to our fa- thers: and to re-
fa- thers, _ to our fa- thers: and to re-mem-
- form the mer- cy prom-is- ed to our fa- thers: and to re- mem-ber his ho- ly
fa- thers, to our fa- thers: and to re- mem- ber his ho- ly
40
- mem-ber his ho- - ly cov- e- nant; To per- form the oath which he
- ber his ho- ly cov- e- nant; To per- form the oath which he
cov- e- nant, his cov- e- nant; To per- form the oath which he
cove-nant, his ho- ly cove- nant; To per- form the oath which he
45
sware to our fa- ther A- bra- ham: that he would give us; That
sware to our fa- ther A- bra-ham: that he would give us;
sware to our fa- ther A- bra- ham: that he would give, [would give] us; That we be-
sware to our fa- ther A- bra-ham: that he would give us;
50
we be- ing de- liv- er-ed out of the hands of our en- e- mies, out
That we be- - ing de- liv- er-
- ing de- liv- er- ed out of the hands of our en- e- mies, de-
That we be-

55
of the hands of our en- - e- mies, of our en- e- mies: might serve him,
- ed out of the hands of our en- e- mies: might serve him,
- liv- er- ed out of the hands of our en- e- mies: might serve him, might
- ing de- liv- er- ed out of the hands of our en- - e- mies: might
60
might serve him with- out fear; In ho- li-ness and righ- te-ous-ness be- fore him: all
might serve him with- out fear; In ho- li-ness and righ- te-ous-ness be- fore him:
serve him with- out fear; In ho- li-ness and righ- te-ous-ness be- - fore him,
serve him with- out fear; In ho- li- ness and righ- te-ous-ness be-
65
the days of our life, our life. And thou, child, shalt be call- ed the
all the days of our life. And thou, child, shalt be call- ed the
be- fore him: all the days of our life. And thou, child, shalt be call- ed the
- fore him: all the days of our life. And thou, child, shalt be call- ed the
70
Pro- phet of the Most High: for thou shalt go be- fore the face of the
Pro- phet of the Most High: for thou shalt go be- fore, for thou shalt
Pro- phet of the Most High: for thou shalt go be- fore the
Pro- phet of the Most High: for thou shalt go be- fore the face of the

75
Lord, be- fore the face of the Lord to pre-pare
go be- fore the face of the Lord to pre- pare his ways,
face, be- fore the face of the Lord to
Lord, be- fore the face of the Lord to pre-pare his ways,
80
his ways, to pre- pare his ways; To
to pre-pare his ways, to pre- pare his ways;
pre-pare his ways, to pre- pare his ways; To give
to pre- pare his ways, to pre- pare his ways;
85
give knowl-edge of sal- va- ti- on un- to his peo- ple, un- to his
To give knowl-edge of sal- va- ti-on un- to his peo-
knowl-edge of sal- va- ti- on un- to his peo- ple, un- to his
To give knowl-edge of sal- va- ti- on un- to his
90
peo- ple: for the re- mis- si- on of their sins; Through the
ple: for the re- mis- si- on of their sins; Through the
peo- ple: for the re- mis- si- on of their sins; Through the
peo- ple: for the re- mis- si- on of their sins; Through the

tender mer-cy of our God: where-by the day-spring from on
ten-der mer- cy of our God: where-by the day-spring from on high, spring from
ten-der mer- cy of our God: where- by the day- spring
ten-der mer- cy of our God: where- by the day-spring from on high, spring
95
high hath vis- it- ed us; To give light to them that sit in dark- ness, and in the
on [high] hath vis- it-ed us; To give light to them that sit in dark- ness, and in the
from on high hath vis- it-ed us; To give light to them that sit in dark- ness, and in the
from on high hath vis- it-ed us; To give light to them that sit in dark- ness, and in the
100
shad- ow of death: and to guide our feet in- to the way of peace, and to
shad- ow of death: and to guide our feet in- to the way of peace, and to
shad- ow of death: and to guide our feet in- to the way
shad- ow of death: and to guide our feet in- to the
105
guide our feet in- to the way of peace. Glo- ry be to the
110
Fa- ther, and to the
guide our feet in- to the way of peace. Glo- ry be to the Fa- ther, and to the
of peace, in- to the way of peace. Glo- ry be to the Fa- ther, and to the
way of peace, in- to the way of peace. Glo- ry be to the Fa- ther, and to the

115
Son: and to the Ho-ly Ghost; As it was in the be-gin- ning,
Son: and to the Ho- ly Ghost; As it was in the be- gin-ning, and _ is ___
Son: and to the Ho- ly Ghost; As it was in the be- gin-ning, and is now, ___
Son: and to the Ho- ly Ghost; As it was in the be-gin-ning, and is now,
and is now, ___ and ev- er shall be: world _
now, and is now, and ev- er shall be: world with- out ___
_ [and is now,] and ev- er shall be: world ___ with- out
and is now, and ev- er shall be: world with- out end, and
120
_ with-out end, and ev- er shall be: world with- out end, and ev- er shall
_ end, _ world ___ with- out ___ end, and ev- er shall be: world
end, and ev- er shall be: world with- out end, world with-out end,
ev- er shall be: world ___ with-out end, and ev- er shall be: world with- out end,
125
be, and ev- er shall be: world with- out ___ end. A- - men.
with- out end, world ___ with- out ___ end. A- - - men.
and ev- er shall be: world with- out ___ end. A- - - - men.
world with-out end, world with- out end. A- - - men.

[28] [Te Deum]

CHOIR I
CHOIR II
CHOIR I
Triplex
Contratenor
Tenor
Bassus
We knowl-edge thee to be the Lord.
We knowl-edge thee to be the Lord.
We knowl-edge thee to ___ be the _ Lord.
We knowl-edge thee to be the Lord.
CHOIR II
5
CHOIR I
All the earth doth wor- ship thee: the Fa- ther ev- er- last- ing. To thee all
All the earth doth worship thee: the Fa- ther ev- er- last- ing. To thee all
All the earth doth wor-ship thee: the Fa- ther ev- er- last- ing. To thee all
All the earth doth wor-ship thee: the Fa- ther ev- er- last- ing. To thee all
10
An- gels cry a- loud: the Heavens, and all the Powers there- in.
An- gels cry a- loud: the Heavens, and all the Powers there- in.
An- gels cry a- loud: the Heavens, and all the Powers there- in.
An- gels cry a- loud: the Heavens, and all the Powers there- in.
CHOIR II
15
To thee Cher- u- bin, and Ser- a-phin: con- tin- ual-ly do ___ cry,
To thee Cher- u- bin, and Ser- a-phin: con- tin- ual-ly do ___ cry,
To thee Cher- u- bin, and Ser- a-phin: con- tin- ual-ly do ___ cry,
To thee Cher- u- bin, and Ser- a-phin: con- tin- ual-ly do ___ cry,

CHOIR I
20
Ho- ly, Ho- ly, Ho- ly: Lord God of Sa- ba- oth;
Ho- ly, Ho- ly, Ho- ly: Lord God of Sa- ba-oth;
Ho- ly, Ho- ly, Ho- ly: Lord God of Sa- - ba- oth;
Ho- ly, Ho- ly, Ho- ly: Lord God of Sa- ba-oth;
CHOIR II
25
Ho- ly, Ho- ly,
Ho- ly, Ho- ly,
Ho- ly, Ho- ly,
Ho- ly, Ho- ly,
Ho-ly: Lord God of Sa-ba- oth;
Ho-ly: Lord God of Sa- - ba- oth;
Ho-ly: Lord God of Sa- ba-oth;
Ho-ly: Lord God of Sa- ba-oth;
CHOIR I
30
Heaven and earth are re- plen- ish-ed with the
Heaven and earth are re- plen-ish- ed with the
Hea- ven and earth are re- plen- ish-ed with the _ maj-
Heaven and earth are re- plen-ish- ed with the maj-
maj- es- ty: of thy Glo- ry.
maj- es- ty: of thy Glo- ry.
- es- ty: of thy Glo- ry.
- es- ty: of thy Glo- ry.
CHOIR II
35
The glo- ri- ous com- pa- ny
The glo- ri- ous com- pa-
The glo- ri- ous com- pa- ny
The glo- ri- ous com- pa- ny
of the A- pos- tles: praise thee.
- ny of the A- pos- tles: praise thee.
of the A- pos- tles: praise thee.
of the A- pos- tles: praise thee.
CHOIR I
40
The good-ly fel- low-ship of the
The good-ly fel- low- ship of the
The good-ly fel- low-ship of
The good-ly fel- low- ship of the

CHOIR II
45
Pro- phets: praise thee. The no-ble ar- my of Mar- tyrs: praise thee.
Pro- phets: praise thee. The no-ble ar- my of Mar-tyrs: praise thee.
the Pro- phets: praise thee. The no-ble ar- my of Mar- tyrs: praise thee.
Pro- phets: praise thee. The no-ble ar- my of Mar-tyrs: praise thee.
CHOIR I
50
CHOIR II
The ho- ly Church through-out all the world: doth knowl-edge thee; The Fa-ther: of an
The ho- ly Church through-out all the world: doth knowl-edge thee; The Fa-ther: of an
The ho- ly Church through-out all the world: doth knowl- edge thee; The Fa-ther: of an
The ho- ly Church through-out all the world: doth knowl- edge thee; The Fa-ther: of an
55
CHOIR I
in- fi-nite Maj- es- ty. Thy hon-our- a- ble, true: and on- ly Son;
in- fi- nite Maj- es- ty. Thy hon-our- a- ble, true: and on- ly Son;
in- fi-nite Maj- es- ty. Thy hon-our- a- ble, true: and on- ly Son;
in- fi-nite Maj- es- ty. Thy hon-our- a- ble, true: and on- ly Son;
CHOIR II
60
CHOIR I
The Ho- ly Ghost al- so: be- ing the Com-for- ter. Thou art the King of
The Ho- ly Ghost al- so: be- ing the Com-for- ter. Thou art the King of
The Ho- ly Ghost al- so: be- ing the Com-for- ter. Thou art the King of
The Ho- ly Ghost al- so: be- ing the Com-for- ter. Thou art the King of

65
CHOIR II
Glo- ry: O Christ. Thou art the ev- er- last-ing Son: of the Fa- ther.
Glo- ry: O Christ. Thou art the ev- er- last-ing Son: of the Fa- ther.
Glo- ry: O Christ. Thou_ art the ev- er- last-ing Son: of the_____ Fa- ther.
Glo- ry: O Christ. Thou. art the ev- er- last-ing Son: of the Fa- ther.
CHOIR I
70
When thou tookst up- on thee to de- liv- er man: thou didst not ab- hor the Vir-gin's
When thou tookst up- on thee to de- liv- er man: thou didst not ab- hor the Vir-gin's
When thou tookst up- on thee to de- liv- er man: thou didst not ab- hor the Vir-gin's
When thou tookst up- on thee to de- liv- er man: thou didst not ab- hor the Vir-gin's
CHOIR II
75
womb. When thou hadst o- ver-come the sharp-ness of death: thou didst o- pen the
womb. When thou hadst o- ver-come the sharp-ness of death: thou didst o- pen the
womb. When thou hadst o- ver-come the sharp-ness of death: thou didst o- pen the
womb. When thou hadst o- ver-come the sharp-ness of death: thou didst o- pen the
80
CHOIR I
King-dom of Heaven to all be- liev- ers. Thou sittst on the right hand of
King-dom of Heaven to all be- liev- ers. Thou sittst on the right hand of
King-dom of Heaven to all be- liev- ers. Thou sittst on the right hand of
King-dom of Heaven to all be- liev- ers. Thou sittst on the right hand of

85
CHOIR II
90
God: in the Glo-ry of the Fa- ther. We be-lieve that thou shall be come: to be our Judge.
God: in the Glo-ry of the Fa- ther. We be-lieve that thou shall be come: to be our Judge.
God: in the Glo-ry of the Fa- ther. We be-lieve that thou shall be come: to be our Judge.
God: in the Glo-ry of the Fa- ther. We be-lieve that thou shall be come: to be our Judge.
CHOIR I
95
We there-fore pray thee, help thy ser- vants: whom thou hast re- deem-ed with thy
We there-fore pray thee, help thy ser-vants: whom thou hast re- deem-ed with thy
We there-fore pray thee, help thy ser-vants: whom thou hast re- deem-ed with thy
We there-fore pray thee, help thy ser- vants: whom thou hast re- deem-ed with thy pre-
CHOIR II
100
pre- ci- ous blood. Make them to be num-bered with thy Saints: in glo- ry ev- er-
pre- ci- ous blood. Make them to be num-bered with thy Saints: in glo- ry ev- er- last-
pre-cious blood. Make them to be num-bered with thy Saints: in glo- ry ev- er- last-
- cious blood. Make them to be num-bered with thy Saints: in glo- ry ev- er-
CHOIR I
CHOIR II
105
- last- ing. and bless thine her- i- tage. Gov-ern them: and
- ing. O Lord, save thy peo- ple: and bless thine her- i- tage. Gov- ern them: and
- ing. and bless thine her- i- tage. Gov-ern them: and
- last- ing. O Lord, save thy peo- ple: and bless thine her- i- tage. Gov-ern them: and

CHOIR I
110
CHOIR II
lift them up for ev- er. Day by day: we mag- ni-fy thee; And we wor-ship thy Name: ev-er
lift them up for ev- er. Day by day: we mag- ni- fy thee; And we wor-ship thy Name: ev-er
lift them up for ev- er. Day by day: _ we mag-ni- fy thee; And we wor-ship thy Name: ev-er
lift them up for ev- er. Day by day: we mag- ni- fy thee; And we wor-ship thy Name: ev-er
CHOIR I
115
world with- out end. Vouch-safe, O Lord: to keep us this day with-
world with- out end. Vouch-safe, O Lord: to keep us this day with-
world with- out end. Vouch-safe, O Lord: to keep us this day with-
world with- out end. Vouch-safe, O Lord: to keep us this day with-
CHOIR II
120
- out ___ sin. O Lord, have mer-cy up- on us: have mer- cy up- on us.
- out sin. O Lord, have mer-cy up- on us: have _____ mer- cy up-on us.
- out sin. O Lord, have mer-cy up- on us: have mer- cy up- on us.
- out sin. O Lord, have mer-cy up- on us: have mer-cy up-on us.
CHOIR I
125
O Lord, let thy mer- cy light-en up- on us: as our trust is in thee.
O Lord, let thy mer- cy light-en up- on us: as our trust is in thee.
O Lord, let thy mer- cy light- en up- on us: as our trust is in thee.
O Lord, let thy mer- cy light- en up- on us: as our trust is in thee.

CHOIR I, II
130
135
O Lord, in thee have I trust- ed: let me nev-er be con- found- ed.
O Lord, in thee have I trust- ed, trust- ed: let me nev-er be con- found- ed, con- found- ed.
O Lord, in thee have I trust- ed: let me nev-er be con-found- ed.
O Lord, in thee have I trust- ed: let me nev-er be con- found- ed.

[29] [Nunc dimittis]

Triplex
Contratenor
Tenor
Bassus
Lord, now let- test thou thy ser- vant de- part in
Lord, now let- test thou thy ser- vant de- part in
Lord, now let- test thou thy ser- vant de- part in
Lord, now let- test thou thy ser- vant de- part in
5
peace: ac- cord- ing to thy word,
peace: ac- cord- ing to thy word,
peace: ac- cord- ing to thy word, ac- cord-
peace: ac- cord- - ing to thy word, ac- cord- ing

10
ac- cord- ing to thy word.
ac- cord- ing to thy word. For mine eyes have
- ing to thy word, ac- cord-ing to thy word. For mine eyes have
to thy word, ac- cord- - ing to thy word. For mine eyes have seen
15
20
seen thy sal- va- ti- on, Which thou hast pre- par-
seen thy sal- va- ti- on, Which thou hast pre- par- ed be-
thy sal- va- ti- on, Which thou hast pre- par- ed be- fore the
25
To be a light to light- en
- ed be- fore the face of all peo- ple; To be a light to light-
- fore the face of all peo- ple, of all peo- ple; To be a light
face, be- fore the face of all peo- ple; To be a light to
the Gen- tiles: and to be the glo- ry of
- en the Gen- tiles: and to be the glo- ry of thy
to light- en the Gen- tiles: and to be the
light- en the Gen- tiles: and to be the glo- ry of thy

30
thy people Is- ra- el. Glo- ry be to the Fa- ther, and to the
peo-ple, of thy peo-ple Is- ra- el. Glo- ry be to the Fa- ther, and to the
glo- ry of thy peo-ple Is- ra- el. Glo- ry be to the Fa- ther, and to the
peo-ple, of thy peo-ple Is- ra- el. Glo- ry be to the Fa- ther, and to the
35
40
Son: and to the Ho- ly Ghost; As it was in the be- gin- ning, is now,
Son: and to the Ho- ly Ghost; As it was in the be-gin- ning, is now,
Son: and to the Ho- ly Ghost; As it was in the be- gin- ning, is now,
Son: and to the Ho- ly Ghost; As it was in the be- gin- ning, is now,
45
and ev- er shall be,
and ev- er shall be, and ev- er
and ev- er shall be: world with- out end, and ev- er shall
and ev- er shall be: world with- out end, and ev- er shall be:
and ev- - er shall be: world with- out end. A- men.
shall be, and ev- er shall be: world with-out end. A- men.
be: world with- out end. A- - men.
world with- out end. A- - men.

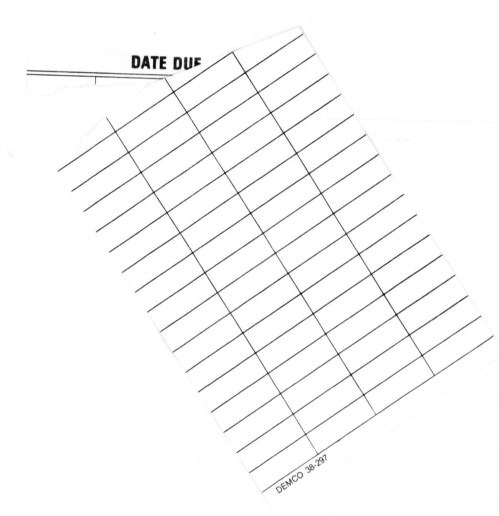